SLOW BURN

SLOW

Sabina Murray

Ballantine Books · New York

BURN

An Available Press Book
Published by Ballantine Books

LIBRARY OF CONGRESS CATALOG CARD NUMBER: 89-91505

ISBN: 0-345-36773-1

Design by Beth Tondreau Design/Jane Treuhaft
Cover design by James R. Harris
Cover photograph: The Image Bank/© 1985 Jurgen Schmitt
Manufactured in the United States of America

First Edition: July 1990
10 9 8 7 6 5 4 3 2 1

SLOW BURN

1

I've heard them talk about mountain climbing. It was popular about ten years ago. There were mountain-climbing weekends when people kept cabins in Ilocos Norte and Benguet and invited friends and relatives to join them. Dressed in hiking outfits, the climbers made their way to the summit, or as far as could be walked without much effort. They broke for lunch around noon. Servants who had carried the baskets of cured meat and fruit up the mountainside set out the food and plates and silverware on large checkered blankets, and everyone sat down and ate. For most, the hiking endeavor ended here. Drinking and eating in the clean mountain air was a far more pleasant way of spending an afternoon than dragging oneself, puffing and probably drenched with perspiration, to the top of a mountain. The younger and stronger men and women persevered, and often made it to the top. The popularity of mountain climbing has since declined. Now people prefer to haunt the nightclubs of Makati Avenue and Manila, and on a more civilized note, the ballet and opera. It seems more worthwhile, because from the top of a mountain, one can see everything, but is seen by no one. I often wonder what it would have been like to be with the mountain climbers. I go to nightclubs.

I was at Euphoria with Eduardo. The sound of the gossiping, drinking, and laughter drifted out to us in waves. I could hardly move, there were so many people. The air was thick with smoke and we were all somehow frozen in the haze. A multitude of perfumes mixed with smoke, and underneath it all, I could detect the scent of fabric damp with perspiration. Lights flashed around us, off the dance floor, in the smoke, on the faces of the people. I didn't see anyone I knew, but everyone looked familiar, the same. It was easy to lose someone in a crowd like that. I stood on the edge, watching, then I pushed my way in.

Eduardo was gripping my wrist firmly. Then he got ahead of me. He was dragging me into people. A woman spilled her drink, cold and sticky, on my arm, and glared after me. Eduardo pushed through happy gossiping groups, and into conversations. I stumbled after him clumsily. We moved onto the perimeter of the dance floor. He plunged in, dodging under arms and around cigarettes, and I followed, hitting every limb and hand he'd managed to avoid. I made quick apologies to couples as I passed. I tried wrenching my hand free, but I couldn't, and then I realized that I hated him. I hated Eduardo.

He saw a booth where his friends were sitting.

"Eduardo, Isobel!" they called in happy chorus.

I found myself squeezed between Eduardo and Monching, a large Chinese mestizo. Monching was smoking a cigar.

"Drinks?" he asked. Smoke spilled out of his mouth. He looked around the table, smiling benignly. "Isobel, what will you have to drink?"

"Double vodka tonic, no ice."

He nodded in approval, his face drawn into a tight smile.

"Eddie?" he asked.

"The same." Eduardo's eyes started searching around the room.

"What are you looking for?" I asked.

"Nothing." Always nothing. He was looking across the room at Antonia de Leon. She was wearing a white blouse and a long silky skirt. Her hair was carefully smoothed back into a barrette, no strand out of place. Her beige evening purse matched her low-heeled shoes. I could hear her shrill laughter over the clinking glasses, over the low chatter and the music coming from the dance floor. She looked as prim and as innocent as she did when we were in school. I pushed my hair out of my face to light a cigarette, then risked another look. Antonia was looking straight at me. We held each other's gaze, maybe for just a moment, maybe for a few seconds, and then she looked down, embarrassed. She looked at her feet, then smiled at her friends. I knew she was uncomfortable. I turned to Eduardo, who was also looking at her.

"Do you know her?" I asked.

"I met her at a party once," he said.

"I went to school with her. She always had the maid carry her books to the classroom."

"She's very rich," he said, nodding, "and quite a prize. Old money like that, both parents so well recognized. Blue blood is hard to come by."

I looked straight at her, biting my lower lip, a little stunned and hurt by Eduardo's last remark. He was even less sensitive than usual.

"Yes, she is well placed," I said, staring down at my hands, watching the ashes slowly form at the end of my cigarette.

"And she's pretty, too," he added.

Our little group fell strangely quiet. They watched us, straight-faced, but inside I knew each one was smiling, even Monching, who loved me. I was down, and they sat around the table, still, watching, while their minds circled like birds of prey.

"She is pretty," I said, looking back to my cigarette, "in a rather doll-like way." I looked around the table waiting for someone to contest this.

"Are you jealous, Isobel?" Eduardo asked me. He sat back comfortably, but careful not to slouch.

"No." I said. I pushed my hair away from my face again and smiled strongly at the others.

"I think you are. It's a problem with women. I don't think any of you are really secure." He took a cigarette from a gold case and tapped it casually on the table.

I looked back at Antonia. She seemed very happy. Her high-pitched laughter reached me across the room, resonating on my ears like drops of rain on a tin roof. She was standing with a tall dark man, Paulo something. Paulo Aguilar. I desperately tried to recall when I had met him, he seemed so familiar. I realized I never had. His father was the leader of the opposition, possibly the next president. He had been pointed out to me at numerous gatherings as a "catch," someone not to be taken lightly. I looked back at Antonia, who was still laughing while she toyed with a lace fan.

"I think you're just as insecure as I am, Eduardo," I ventured boldly, "and I think you can be jealous."

"Oh really?" he said. There was an uneasy feeling all around the table. Eduardo's mouth tightened, and still he played with his cigarette. He tapped it first with the left hand and then with the right. Everyone was waiting for Eduardo to say something, to put me back in my place.

"You're very cocky tonight," said Eduardo. "You seem to be forgetting that you're with nice people."

Monching opened his mouth, but said nothing, then went back to puffing on his cigar. I decided I had to leave.

"Excuse me," I said to the group, then pushed past Eduardo and out onto the perimeter of the dance floor. A short distance away stood Antonia with Paulo Aguilar. Paulo. I could feel the eyes of the people I had just left watching me, trying to predict my next move. I stood, arms folded in front, unsure of just what to do. Then I heard Eduardo's voice.

"Isobel, what are you doing?" He was laughing.

I walked quickly across the corner of the dance floor, toward Antonia and her little group. Strangely drawn to Paulo, I glanced up quickly. He was watching me. I looked down at the floor, at the tops of people's shoes, then I moved quickly toward him, not knowing what to do, not sure of myself, or of anything, though I was conscious of Eduardo and Monching and those vultures watching me. I was getting closer, dodging people, dodging cigarettes. I was hurrying, although I wasn't sure why. Then he was there in front of me, Paulo, Paulo Aguilar. I looked quickly to his left and suddenly spilled my drink over the front of his shirt.

I heard laughter at the table. It was a wonderful joke to them, my spilling the drink. A funny accident. On Paulo Aguilar. In the middle of Euphoria. An amusing incident to all, except Eduardo, who watched, sulking, because only Eduardo knew what had just happened. Only he knew that he had just lost me.

The evening had become a blur of drinks and more drinks, cigarettes, and I think a few joints, maybe. I remember standing with my face against the fine linen of Paulo's shirt. He was talking to people, over the top of my head, but I rested there, my eyes half-closed. All I saw was the button of his shirt, the third button. I could feel his warmth coming through the fabric, and I felt very secure.

"Do you want another drink?" he asked. His voice vibrated deeply through his chest. I shook my head.

"Paulo," I heard a woman say, "who is your friend?"

"Isobel," he answered. "She spilled a drink on me."

He nodded in agreement to some question. I don't know what. Then we left the area of the disco and went upstairs.

I woke up in the hotel room at around 5:30 A.M., maybe only two hours after I had gone to sleep. I was so dehydrated that my tongue had swollen and was sticking to the roof of my mouth. Pale light was filtering through the blinds, making vague checkered patterns on the floor. Paulo was next to me, breathing regularly, his dark head resting on the pillow. I was certain I did not look that peaceful when I slept. I got up from the bed and went to the window.

A slow burning sun was rising over Manila.

Somewhere, fighting cocks, one foot tied to a chair, had started scratching in the ground and had started to crow. Children gathered bread in large baskets and made their way, shouting "*pan de sal*" through the cool streets and alleyways.

A maid, standing at a gate, gave the bread boy a few pesos. He handed her back a small brown paper bag, full of warm rolls. She entered the house to make breakfast, but first prepared a cup of coffee for the mistress, my mother, who would soon be on her way to Mass.

My mother was upstairs, putting on a crisp white dress with a blue sash. She then picked up her fan, a neatly folded veil, and a set of rosary beads, and put them in a perfectly white embroidered purse. Before she left the room she paused before the mirror. Slim and straight and handsome. She turned to leave, taking one last glance to see that her hair had been well smoothed into her bun, and then went down to the kitchen. Her low heels clicked on the wood floors as she tried to make her way quietly past the other rooms, but in the first two, no one stirred, and in the third, no one was there.

2

I took a taxi and got home around eight A.M. The maid let me in, smiling coyly. I chose to ignore it. I had a headache, and my mind felt cold and dull. I walked quickly past the hall mirror, heels clicking on the marble, and stopped at the foot of the stairs. A door closed upstairs, and I heard someone walking down the hallway in slippers. It was my sister, Lourdes, who had just woken up.

"Isobel," she said, pushing her hair out of her face.

"Hello," I answered. She was looking at my dress.

"When did you get in?" she asked.

"Just now." I smiled condescendingly, as if this could somehow justify my appearance.

"Where were you?"

"I was at Euphoria with old friends. I lost track of the time."

"Eduardo called here at around 7:30. He wanted to know where you were. I said that you were asleep."

"I never knew Eduardo to get up before nine." I laughed, maybe too flippantly. A wall was growing between us.

"He wanted to know where you were," she repeated.

"Eduardo asks too many questions."

Lourdes turned around and walked back to her room, closing the door loudly behind her. For one moment I thought I felt a pang of guilt, but it was just irritation. I decided not to feel sorry for myself, not just then, and went up to my room to shower and dress for Mass. Mass started at noon.

It was very hot that day, and I sat in church, patting the perspiration off my forehead, cursing myself for forgetting a fan. The woman seated beside me had remembered hers, a large embroidered one, which she kept opening and closing, rattling it like a weapon. She, and all the other women in the church, clung tightly to their fans, batting futilely at the still-damp air.

"My friends," said the priest, "we must look for leaders in these coming elections. Do not count on personal relations. . . ."

It seemed as if he had been speaking for hours.

Two pews in front of me, I spotted Jorge della Cruz. His thick neck was covered with beads of perspiration. He kept glaring up at the oscillating fan as if a look could redirect its path. Jorge was my friend and I had news for him. Maybe he had some gossip for me. I got up from my seat, earning a look of disapproval from the woman with the fan, and walked up and out the north transept door. Jorge followed close behind. We sat on a bench a short distance from the church. He took my hand and kissed it lightly.

"Jorge, where is your wife?" I asked him. I was feeling mischievous.

"She's at her parents' this weekend," he answered, smiling.

"Is that why I saw you at Euphoria last night?"

"Maybe," he answered, "and maybe I saw you having too good a time."

I laughed.

"Well," I said, "how has the domestic life been?"

"Domestic." He shook his head. "The maid!" he said, suddenly animated. "We thought she had been possessed. She was saying the Lord's Prayer backward in the laundry room."

"What did you do?" I asked.

"I called a priest. He came into the house with his little bottle of holy water, squirted it right in the baby's face. Little Jorge was screaming, and the priest just marched around the house, chanting in Latin, exorcising all the wrong servants."

"Did it work?" I asked.

"No. My brother-in-law, the doctor, caught the maid having a fit in the middle of the kitchen, and diagnosed it immediately. Epilepsy."

I laughed.

"Is there anything new with you? Anything I should know about?"

"No," I said. "Nothing much, but I went to see Manang Josepina the other day. And she told me that a tall dark man was going to walk into my life, and last night he did."

"Paulo Aguilar?"

I nodded.

"You know, he's a friend of mine."

"I knew that," I said.

"He wants to see you again." Jorge smiled. "The ballet this Wednesday. Are you free?"

"Wednesday?"

"Yes. I'll pick you up at around eight."

"Eight is fine," I said.

"Good."

"But what about Rosario?" I asked.

"Rosario," he said, "will stay home with the baby."

He seemed to be challenging me to say something else, but I didn't. I felt very glad that I did not have to stay home with the baby.

I was nervous when Wednesday night finally arrived. I argued nonstop with my mother. She told me that I should have stayed with Eduardo, that I couldn't keep a suitor. Eduardo, she said, was in love with me. If I had waited, he might have married me. The thought of Rosario, however, stayed fast in my mind. I was glad to be going to the ballet, no matter how many times my mother mentioned those tired gray years that came to all, even me. I lit a cigarette and looked at my reflection. I was a little too thin, a little too drawn, and my anxious expression was neither engaging nor elegant. I opened the door and yelled to the maid to fix me a drink. My mother was the one who brought it to the door.

"Isobel," she said, "whatever is the matter?"

I looked at her incredulously.

"Get that look off your face, and straighten your neckline," she said.

I stood there, drink in one hand, cigarette in the other, while she straightened the neckline of the dress.

"Who are you going to meet?" she asked.

"Paulo Aguilar. I already told you that."

"Does he like you?"

"He finds me amusing."

"Well, pull yourself together," she said as she left the room. "Jorge will be here any minute now." She closed the door quietly behind her.

Jorge was actually half an hour late, which gave me just enough time to have two more drinks. I met him at the bottom of the stairs, my anxieties numbed.

"Isobel," he said, "that's a beautiful dress."

"Thank you," I said.

"I'm afraid we have to hurry," he said. "We can't miss the start. I don't know where the Aguilars' box is."

I found myself in the back of Jorge's car, feeling very sleepy. Jorge sat beside me, occasionally moving forward to scream things at the driver, then he moved back again.

"We're taking a short cut," he said.

We left the tall buildings and wide streets and took a narrow one-way road behind apartments and auto-body shops. Soon we were zigzagging through narrow alleyways and hovels in a part of town I didn't recognize. I had never been there. Jorge kept looking at his watch and shouting at the driver, who at this point was shouting back. I just sat, complacently, feeling the effect of the alcohol wear off, my eyes focused on nothing in particular.

Suddenly the driver jammed on the brakes, and I

found myself thrown into the well of the car with my legs folded beneath me. The driver leaped out and started screaming something about a stupid kid. Jorge got out of the car. He walked slowly to the front, saying nothing, shaking his head. I pulled myself up, back onto the seat of the car, trying to orient myself.

"Jorge," I called, "what is it?"

"Isobel, just stay in the car," he said.

I opened the door and walked slowly around to the driver's side. The broken body of a small boy lay just a short distance from the car. The headlights were shining right on him.

"Isobel!" Jorge shouted. I had no idea how long he had been calling me. "Isobel, get back in the car."

"Jorge," I said, "take me home."

"Take you home? I can't do that."

"Why not? Take me home."

"We're going to be late," he said as he helped me into the car.

"Jorge, I don't want to go."

He took my hand.

"We have obligations," he said. "We have to go. And besides, we didn't kill him. His body was cold. He was already dead. We just hit the body."

"You're lying," I said.

"I'm not lying."

I looked at him blankly.

"I'm not lying!" Then he turned to the driver. "Hurry up, but for God's sake, be careful."

The driver backed up from the body and drove around it. There was silence in the car. A few short minutes later, we were at the Cultural Center. The car turned up the long elevated driveway and pulled over to the curb. A uniformed guard walked over and opened my door, but I sat, immobile. Jorge jumped out of the car and ran around to my side.

"Isobel!" he said, now angry. "What are you doing?"

"I want to go home," I answered, not looking at him.

He grabbed my upper arm.

"I don't care about me," he said, "but I'm not going to sit by and watch you do this to yourself. Paulo is waiting, somewhere in there, while you sit in this car like a simpering fool."

I looked him straight in the face.

"We killed someone."

Jorge let go of my arm and took two steps back.

"You're going to regret this," he said.

I felt my resolution waver. Paulo would be waiting, and Paulo did not care. Paulo did not like me because I was softhearted, but because I had a ready laugh.

I sat pensively.

"Isobel," said Jorge coaxingly, "the performance will start soon."

I stepped slowly out of the car and took Jorge's arm. My mind was spinning, but I managed to calm myself. I wondered at my ability to move and speak and smile. Then I saw Paulo moving toward us across the room, and I knew, somehow, that I had made the right decision.

3

Holding Jorge's arm was reassuring that evening. The whole room was a swirling sea of sequins, smoke, and perfume. Paulo advanced toward us, waving people aside, politely avoiding conversations, and there I stood, firmly anchored to Jorge, convinced that if I let go, I would be swept around the room.

"Do you find him attractive?" Jorge whispered.

"Paulo? I don't know."

Paulo had been detained by a group of elderly women with carefully coiffed buns and layers of makeup. They fussed over him as he looked around, bored.

"Some girls find him handsome," Jorge continued.

"I think I'm scared of him."

"Scared?" Jorge laughed. He raised his lighter to my cigarette. I didn't remember having put it in my mouth in the first place.

"Do I have time for a drink?" I asked.

"No," said Jorge. And then Paulo was with us. I said good evening and smiled.

"Isobel," he said, "that's a beautiful dress."

I think I said thank you. Maybe I smiled.

"Jorge," Paulo said, and they shook hands. They looked as if they had just completed a business transaction. I transferred myself from Jorge's arm to Paulo's arm. Jorge walked off, presumably to the bar, and I watched the sea of people close densely behind him.

"Isobel, we should get to the box. The performance will start in just a few minutes." Paulo started leading me up the marble stairs. "I wish we had time for a drink," he said apologetically.

"Well, it's our fault." I said. "You see, we hit a dog on the way here. It delayed us."

"A dog?" he said. "How unpleasant."

The lights suddenly dimmed, and the music started softly floating up from the orchestra. I was imagining how that poor creature had looked, but the music was strengthening, and there was now a lonely dancer on the stage. I found all my unpleasant thoughts, even the false ones, melt away.

I was mesmerized by the ballet, not because it was particulary good, but ballets always have this effect on me. The dancers perform their parts in perfect time, and always with that sweet music and clear light. Sometimes the dance becomes violent, passionate, and the stage is covered with energetic, tense, and vibrant bodies. I feel like God viewing the world in miniature. I watched as the prima ballerina turned slow circles with the support of her partner. He caught her as she fell gracefully to the left. I wondered what would happen should he become distracted and fail to catch her. I looked over at Paulo, who was looking at where my dress met my leg, just above the knee.

"Do you like the ballet?" I asked him.

"No, not really." He smiled at me.

Afterward, I ran into Jorge as I was coming out of the powder room. Paulo was standing a short distance away, with his back to us, talking to a group of men. Jorge grabbed my arm and took me to stand right beside a large indoor plant.

"Well, how was it?" he asked.

"Jorge, I really don't know. I asked him if he liked the ballet, and he said he didn't."

"That was all?"

I nodded.

"Intermission?"

"We had a few drinks," I said.

"Should I take you home?"

I shrugged my shoulders.

Paulo had finished his conversation and was walking quickly toward us.

"Hello," he said as he nodded in Jorge's direction. Jorge let go of my arm and smiled.

"I'm going home now," he said.

"Isobel and I are going for a few drinks. You're welcome to join us," said Paulo.

"I'd love to," Jorge replied, throwing his arms up in a gesture of total despair, "but I have a wife"—he waved his forefinger at Paulo—"and a baby."

And then Jorge was gone, and it was just Paulo and me in a room full of people.

"Tap Room?" he suggested. I agreed, and we walked down the stairs and out to the drive. I could see all the way to the bay, where the lights on the yachts twinkled as they bobbed on the soft waves.

"It's pretty out there," I said, gesturing with my cigarette.

"And if you were out there, you would see the lights lining the drive to the Cultural Center"—he made an arc with his hands—"and you would say how pretty it was here."

"I probably would," I agreed. "But you can't see where you're standing. You can only see what is far away. If I was to say, 'How beautiful the lights are here at the Cultural Center,' you'd think I was absurd."

"I would," he said. His car pulled up, a black limousine, and he opened the back door for me.

"My father's," he said apologetically.

Soon we were at the Manila Hotel. He led me through the lobby to the Tap Room, where we were seated at a booth near the door. I casually lit my cigarette.

"Paulo, why did you bring me to the ballet if you don't like it?"

"I love the ballet. I just don't like ballet." He turned to address the waitress.

"For the lady . . ."

"A vodka tonic," I said.

"And I'll have whatever that man over there is drinking," he said. He pointed at a green drink in what looked like a goldfish bowl. It belonged to an Iranian who sat by himself at the bar.

"I think it's a Singapore Sling," I said. "Do you like sweet drinks?"

"Not really," he answered.

"Why did you order it?"

"It's a fascination with what other people have." He smiled strangely.

"Drinks?"

"Drinks, cars"—he paused to light a cigarette—"sometimes women."

I was a little stunned. He seemed to think he was paying me a compliment.

"Why did you leave Eduardo Arguelles?" Paulo said, smiling. "I heard he was very fond of you."

I had no ready answer. I racked my brain, but there was absolutely nothing there.

"He was too short."

"Isobel," he said, "you have no conscience." Paulo was very amused, and seemed to mean it as another compliment.

"Are you impressed?" I asked.

"Yes," he said, "I am impressed. I admire that."

I stared at him blankly. The conversation was frustrating me. Paulo looked at me, smiling oddly, as I desperately searched for something to talk about. Gossip? He would be bored. Politics would be too touchy an issue. Past women would be inappropriate. I didn't know him well enough. Travel. I tried to think of someplace I'd been recently that would interest him. San Francisco maybe.

"Isobel, you look distressed," he said.

"No, no," I told him. "Just waiting for my drink."

The waitress brought our drinks over, mine simple and clear in a Tom Collins glass with a large wedge of lime, his green, immense, with a paper parasol. I took a gulp out of the glass and smiled at him, as if the drink had caused a significant change in my condition. Paulo slouched deeply into his chair and watched me surreptitiously.

"Isobel, I'm twenty-seven. Do you think that's old?"

"Of course not," I answered. "I've had older friends than that."

Paulo started laughing, and I realized how incriminating that last statement had sounded. I felt my face was glowing. I reached for my drink.

"You are very funny," he said. He was swinging his knee underneath the table as he said this, intentionally hitting my foot. "Let's go," he said, standing up.

"Where?" I asked.

"Upstairs." He raised both his eyebrows. I remained seated.

"To see the view," he suggested. He took my hand.

"All right," I said. I was relieved that we wouldn't have to talk anymore.

I got home early, at around two A.M. I had hoped that everyone would be asleep when I got there, but I could hear the clicking of a typewriter echoing down the stairs from Lourdes's room. I tiptoed along the hallway and past her room, opening my door quietly. The typing stopped.

"Isobel?" she said, in a loud whisper.

"Yes," I answered. But she didn't say anything else, just resumed typing. I wondered if our relationship would have been any better if she wasn't so plain.

I woke up at ten, stayed in bed until eleven, and was dressed at twelve. I walked down the hallway, trying to think of what I wanted to eat and whether I should have breakfast or lunch. The door to my mother's room was open just a crack.

"Mother?" I whispered.

"Come in."

The curtains were still pulled, and she was lying in bed.

"Mother, where's Tito Mando?" Tito Mando was my mother's husband, Lourdes's father, but no relative of mine.

"He's in the province. His mother, they think she's dying."

"Again?"

My mother looked confused.

"Mother," I said as I took a cigarette from the pack on her dresser, "she's always dying."

I sat by the chair near her bed.

"Aren't you getting up today?" I asked.

She shook her head.

"You know," I said, "we have that baptism at three."

"I can't go," she said, shaking her head. "I don't feel well."

"Are you sick?" I asked her.

"I, well, yes, I'm sick. Can you get me my cigarettes?"

I brought them over, sat down, and held her hand.

"You know, Tito Vince wanted you to come." Tito Vince was my father.

"No," she said, "I'm not going." Tears started to well up in her eyes, and I dropped the issue. I squeezed her hand, so small and fine. We were silent for some time, while the darkness crept around us.

"Do you want to hear about the ballet?" I asked. She nodded.

"Well," I started, "Marietta had her tiara on again. So beautiful a tiara, and such an ugly face . . ."

4

I intentionally dressed inappropriately for the baptism. Anticipating yards of patterned cottons and finely embroidered blouses, I put on a tight-fitting, black linen dress with brass buttons running all the way down the front. I pulled my hair tightly off of my face and fixed it into a bun. In all this severity, I looked oddly like my mother.

I arrived at the house at around 3:30, not really knowing what to expect. Meetings with my half-sisters on my father's side were always interesting. They viewed me with distaste, but at the same time, envy. I was my father's youngest child, and he looked upon me with more affection and love than any of my older siblings could inspire.

"Tito Vince!" I called as I got out of the car. I ran over to him, and he took my hands and smiled at me.

"Isobel!"

I kissed him on the cheek.

"How very like your mother you look," he said.

"And how handsome you look. Not at all like a man with two grandchildren."

"Are you alone?" He looked in the direction of the car.

"Yes," I said apologetically. "She's sick."

"That's too bad. I'd like to see her." He seemed suddenly sad.

"You'll see her." I smiled. "That Mando is such an ass. He's in the province with his mother, again."

"I'll arrange something," he said. "But how are you, Isobel. How are things with you?"

"I have a new boyfriend. Paulo Aguilar."

"Aguilar?" My father nodded in approval. "And what of Arguelles?"

"I don't know." I shrugged my shoulders.

My father laughed.

"Meet me in the library in half an hour, and I'll give you some money," he said, winking.

I noticed my three sisters in the lanai, looking at us sour-faced. I left my father, rushing off to the bar, and ordered two drinks, then went to the bathroom. I really did look like my mother. My hair was neat, my makeup still flawless. I bolted down the first drink and, taking the second, walked out to the lounge. Rosita Villar was sitting there alone, smoking. I felt sure she had been waiting for me.

"Isobel!" she said, running over. She kissed me on both cheeks and took my arm. "How are you?"

"I'm fine, Rosita. How are you?"

"Very well," she said quickly. "I talked to Eduardo's sister the other day. She said that the two of you had had a . . . a fight."

"Yes," I said, nodding.

"And now," she continued, "you have found friendship with Paulo Aguilar."

I looked at her straight in the eyes, slowly pulling my arm from her grasp.

"I have met Paulo," I said.

"Well, Paulo," she pursued, "how is he?"

"As a lover?" I asked. Poor Rosita. Poor, thin, dark, ugly Rosita. She had taken two steps back. Her large teeth rested on her lower lip. I had clearly shocked her.

"No, no. Of course not," she said.

"Rosita . . ." I continued, teasing.

She turned and started walking out the door.

"He's good, Rosita!" I shouted. "He's very very good!"

A couple exiting the dining room looked at me, a

little confused. I stood there, empty glass in hand, laughing uncontrollably. Rosita. Poor, ugly Rosita.

I decided I needed another drink. I walked out to the bar, imagining what people were saying about me. Maybe they didn't notice me at all, but I imagined that they did, and what they were saying: "Look at that dress," or "How she looks like her mother."

I saw my father's wife, Carmella, sitting in her wheelchair by the poolside. A maid in a white starched uniform and nurses' cap was in attendance.

"Tita Carmella," I said. I went over and kissed her cheek. It was like a slab of fat on her face. "How are you? How is the gout?"

She said nothing, but looked at me as if to say, "You are my gout." I walked a short distance away and lit a cigarette, feeling her eyes burn on my back. Little Marco, my four-year-old nephew, ran by me, and I grabbed him around the waist.

"Marco," I said, "Who is your favourite tita?"

"You are, Tita Isobel."

"Why?"

"Because you're my prettiest tita."

"In the whole world?"

"Yeah," he said.

"I'm going to throw coins off the balcony later," I said, "and I want you to stand in the front row so that I can throw all the coins to you, okay?"

"Okay," he said.

I let him go, and he ran off to join the other children.

"He's very fond of you."

I turned around quickly. It was my half-sister, Melay. She looked at me coldly. She was thirty-two now, unmarried, unhappy. Her broad, angular face was so full of hatred, it frightened me.

"Boys tend to like me," I said, and managed a smile. I walked past her, out to the car, to get the coins to throw for the children, but I changed my mind. I decided it was time to leave. I had been there one hour.

5

Friday, I got a note from Paulo. His driver brought it to the house. It was on a small plain sheet of paper, and his writing was barely legible.

> Isobel,
> Sorry I haven't called. I can't. Next weekend (the fifteenth?) I've organized a get-together with some close friends at our "chalet" in Baguio. I hope you can come. I've arranged the whole thing just for you.
> Paulo

I folded the note and stood in the hallway, not

knowing whether to be insulted or flattered. Today, I was truly alone in the house. Lourdes was at school. Mother was in the province with her husband. Apparently Mando's mother really was dying. I had looked forward to a day like this when I could spend quiet time alone, but I was thinking too much. I decided that I had to leave the house as soon as possible. I called up Jorge.

"Jorge! Let's meet somewhere for coffee," I suggested.

"I can't," he said, "but tonight, I was wondering if you needed a ride to the party."

"Party?"

"Yes. Antonia de Leon's. It starts at around eight."

"This is the first I've heard of it."

"But Isobel, I heard you were going."

"From who?"

He was silent.

"Jorge," I said, "I know you're lying. And I know I wasn't invited."

"An error, I'm sure."

"Not an error," I said. "Is Paulo going?"

"Yes, as a matter of fact, he is."

"Then why would Antonia invite me?"

"Actually, Paulo called me," said Jorge. "He wants you there."

"I'm not going," I said.

"Isobel, you should be flattered. You've made Antonia insecure, and Paulo, Paulo doesn't care about it."

"Jorge, don't be ridiculous. Do you know how uncomfortable I would be?"

"Take my arm when we go in. I won't stay long. They'll think I just dropped by to be polite on my way to some other place, with you."

I didn't know what to say.

"What else are you going to do? I'm going to be there. Paulo's going to be there. Where are you going to be? Sitting at home reading a book? Watching TV with the cat on your lap?"

"Okay. Enough," I said. It was very stupid of me to agree to this, but Jorge could talk me into doing anything. He knew me well, well enough to make me resent it.

In the car on the way to Antonia's house, I had this sense of foreboding that something was going to happen to me, and it was going to be Jorge's fault.

"I don't know why you're so worried," he said.

I looked at him coldly.

"Even if you do have reason, which you don't, there will be so many people there, they won't even notice you."

This sounded a little more convincing. We pulled up to the house. There weren't that many cars parked out front, but I didn't allow myself to dwell on this.

I walked in bravely, holding on to Jorge's arm. It was too quiet. There was no one there. Antonia was with a small group of men. She was laughing as usual, but it sounded forced and nervous. I spotted Paulo sitting in an armchair by himself, nursing a tall orange drink.

"There's Paulo," I said, and began to walk over. I didn't get very far. Standing by the peanuts was Eduardo. I watched him, frozen in my place, until he saw me. We were both caught off guard and stood there, not knowing what to do. Eduardo looked angry. I knew that I was flushed, embarrassed. Out of the corner of my eye I could see people had noticed the awkward situation. The room was becoming quiet. I turned around and walked to the bathroom, which turned out to be the kitchen, where there seemed to be a million people. I escaped through the next door that presented itself, a screen door, and discovered that I was standing outside, behind the garage, a short distance from a large garbage can. I found my cigarettes, with some difficulty, and lit one. Noises from the party grew louder, muted music and soft chatter drifting out. I felt safe in the dark. I heard the clang of metal on concrete and turned to see a very thin cat going through the garbage. She picked through the trash, delicately clawing at bits of plastic and paper. Finally, she found a cheese rind, leaped down to the ground, and gnawed hungrily at it.

"Here you are, Isobel."

I turned around quickly. It was Paulo.

"No one could figure out where you'd disappeared to. May I just say that your performance in there was magnificent. There have been few times in my life when I've been so amused."

"Amused?" I asked incredulously.

"Did you see Antonia's face when you walked in?"

"No, I didn't."

"It was as though you were stark naked. And Eduardo . . ." He tilted his head down and smiled mischievously.

"There was absolutely nothing funny about it. I want to leave immediately."

"Of course you do," he said. "And we will."

"Where are we going?"

"Antipolo." He motioned toward the door with his head.

"I'll meet you out front," I said.

I went back into the kitchen. Sitting on the counter was a silver tray loaded down with hors d'oeuvres, crackers with pink salmon paste garnished with sliced black olives. I took three and went outside. My cat was still chewing on her cheese rind. I threw her the crackers. She sniffed one gingerly, but went back to her rind.

"You'll eat it later," I said, "when you're really hungry." Then I went out front to join the others.

Paulo had the engine running. Jorge sat in back, intently studying something in a paper bag. I got in up front. I smelled leather seats, and cologne, and tobacco.

"How long do you think it will take us to get to Antipolo?" I asked.

"Forty-five minutes maximum," said Paulo.

He turned into the street. We rounded the corner with a screech, intended, I'm sure, for the people inside, and soon were on an open highway. Paulo switched on the radio.

"I hate this song," said Jorge. "It's very popular now. You hear it everywhere."

"I like it," said Paulo.

Jorge furrowed his brow.

"I guess it isn't that bad," he said.

I looked at both of them and shook my head.

"Isobel," said Paulo, "take out your hair."

I started to unbraid it, not really questioning why. He reached over with his right hand, tousling it further, then looked down to the control panel and opened all the windows. Wind whipped my hair all around my face, and I started laughing.

"Turn up the radio," Jorge shouted.

Paulo turned it way up. Air and music blasted all around me. I turned around to look at Jorge, keeping the hair out of my face with my hand. Jorge sat back comfortably, singing loudly.

"What's in the bag?" I shouted.

"What?"

I pointed at the paper bag he was holding.

"This?" He held it up.

I nodded.

"Baguio Gold." He smiled. "Good stuff."

I turned to Paulo.

"Did you get it?" I shouted.

"Yes. There's some vodka back there, too."

"Did you plan all of this?" I asked.

"I couldn't stay in that party all night," he said. "People ask too many questions."

I shrugged my shoulders. He grabbed my arm and shook me playfully, then rested his hand on my neck.

"You shift the gears," he said.

We turned up a roadway that soon became gravel. We were nearly there. The air smelled cleaner, and it was cooler. We parked beneath a tree. I got out of the car and looked down at the lights twinkling in the Marikina Valley below.

"This is wonderful," I said, "so clean and natural."

"I need a drink," said Paulo, getting out of the car.

Jorge took a large brown paper bag from the backseat and set it on the hood. He took out a bottle of vodka, a carton of orange juice, three glasses, a pouch of grass, and a pipe. I nodded in approval.

"Isobel, take my jacket," said Paulo. He took it off and handed it to me. Drinks were poured, the pipe was lit, and soon the evening slipped into a timeless, colorless, pointless game. I sat on the hood of the car wrapped up in Paulo's jacket, my hair a tangled mess. Paulo sat beside me, finishing the last of the evening's last drink. Jorge lay on the grass, looking up at the stars.

"There's Marietta's tiara," he said, "there's my car, and my house. There's my first girlfriend."

"Jorge," I asked, "am I up there?"

"Of course you are," he said. "We all are, somewhere. . . ."

I turned to Paulo, who was laughing to himself.

"Private joke?" I asked.

He shook his head.

"No, just thinking about you tonight, and that look on Antonia's face."

"You laugh at everything," I said. "You don't take anything seriously."

He faked a pained look.

"Isobel, I take some things very seriously."

"Like what?" I raised an eyebrow.

"My vices," he said. "I take my vices very seriously."

"And what are they?"

"Isobel," he said, "I have many vices, but you are by far the favorite." I laughed.

"No one has ever called me a vice before," I said. I looked out into the darkness, trying to see Jorge, but it was black. I couldn't see anything, and it was strangely quiet.

"Paulo," I said, "I think we've lost Jorge."

"Well, we can't have that, can we?" he said. "I'll turn the headlights on."

The lights came on, two beams slicing through the darkness, and Jorge's outline was revealed. He was urinating beside a tree. I started laughing hysterically. Paulo smiled and shook his head, and Jorge, realizing that he had been discovered, simply turned his back to us and finished his business. I sat on the hood of the car, nursing the pipe. I hummed softly, feeling tired and happy, looking down at the twinkling lights in the valley below, and I asked myself, Shouldn't we be somewhere?

I left for Baguio at around noon the following Thursday. I'd planned to leave at eight, in order to arrive with the other guests, but Jorge called and demanded that I have coffee with him before I left. He said that it was very unfair of Paulo to take me away for an entire weekend, especially when Paulo knew that he, Jorge, couldn't come. We had gotten back from Antipolo at six in the morning, and Jorge's wife was furious. Her anger turned to tears, which melted Jorge's heart. He was consumed with guilt for almost four days. He was home for dinner, and kind and attentive to Rosario and the baby, but the thought of a barren weekend was more than he could bear. He spent the entire time at Café Adriatico telling me how miserable his life was, but I held my ground and refused to feel guilty. Sulking, he walked me out to the car.

"Jorge," I said, "it's not that terrible."

He shook his head.

"Good-bye, Isobel," he said.

I kissed his forehead.

"I want you to wish me a good time."

"Have fun," he said, "and say hi to Paulo for me."

I waved and told the driver to go on. I did feel sorry for Jorge, who stood on the sidewalk until we were out of sight. Only Jorge could make me feel this way.

The ride up was long and uneventful. It occurred to me that I hadn't asked Paulo who the other guests were, but I found other things to think about. My mother had gotten very excited over the idea of my weekend in Baguio. We had gone shopping and bought everything from lounging pants to a new toothbrush. She had then left for the province with Mando and his mother, and had left Lourdes in charge of the house. Lourdes would do a good job.

The road zigzagged up the mountain. Occasional avalanches sent small loads of gravel clattering onto the car roof and hood, but this didn't bother me. Soon we reached the city, and then Wright Park. Paulo's place was on Outlook Drive, and was one of the more impressive holiday houses. As I had predicted, I was the last guest to arrive. Paulo met me at the door.

"How was your ride up?" he asked.

"Uneventful," I said. "Why are you smiling like that?"

"Like what?" he asked.

"Like you know something about me."

"Nonsense." He laughed. "Come, I'll show you to your room."

We walked down a long wooden corridor, all the way to the end.

"Your room." He pointed to the right. "And my room." He pointed to the left. "Hurry and freshen up. I know the other guests will be eager to see you. They're in the lounge, sitting around the fireplace."

He sat on the bed watching me fix my hair and powder my face. I could see his reflection in the mirror.

"You've got that look on your face again," I said.

"Don't be ridiculous. Come on," he said, tugging at my sleeve.

I could hear the fire crackling, and happy voices as I went down the hallway. I prepared a wonderful smile and walked into the room. I stopped at the doorway, stunned. Sitting at the fire with the other guests was Eduardo. I turned around and walked back into the hallway.

"Paulo," I said in a loud whisper, "Eduardo is here."

"I know," said Paulo coolly.

"What's he doing here?"

"I invited him."

"You invited him. Why?"

"A political move. It isn't good to have someone mad at you, no matter how good the reason." He held my shoulders. "I'm sorry. I didn't realize you'd be so upset."

"What do you mean? Of course you knew I'd be upset. Why didn't you tell me?"

"Because I knew you wouldn't have come."

"That's true," I said.

I was confused. My head was spinning around and around. I wanted to go somewhere or do something, but I didn't know what to do. I lit a cigarette.

"Isobel," Paulo said, "come in and meet the guests. You can't stand in the hallway all weekend."

I looked at him angrily and walked quickly into the room.

"Anna," I said to the woman seated by the fireplace, "how was Spain? It rained the whole time? That's awful."

Enrique Diaz was seated beside her.

"Enrique, your mother's exhibition was such a success. She must be thrilled. How's your sister? Good."

I saw Gina del Rosario.

"Gina! What a wild woman you've been. I haven't been able to track you down in weeks."

Finally, I turned to Eduardo.

"Eduardo, you look wonderful. What have you been up to?"

He looked at me, slightly disturbed, then ran his fingers through his hair.

"Not much," he said.

I went and took a seat at the far side of the room, resigning myself to the fact that the weekend would be a total disaster. I looked across to the doorway, where Paulo stood, applauding me silently.

Dinner was hell. Paulo sat at the head of the table with me at his left and Eduardo at his right. I was most uncomfortable. Eduardo was staring at me, unashamed, and it was difficult for me to eat. The conversation, which was unbelievably dull, was led by Anna, who spoke endlessly of her time in Spain, which she had spent almost entirely indoors, due to the unpleasant weather.

I reached for the wine and poured myself a glassful.

"Isobel," said Gina, "isn't that your fourth glass?"

"Why, are you counting?" I asked sharply.

I felt Paulo's knee bump mine under the table. He looked at me reproachfully. I looked at Eduardo, who was smiling. I took a gulp out of the glass.

"Why don't we go into the living room?" I suggested.

"Isobel," said Gina, "some people are still eating."

"Well," I said, standing up, "I'm off to have a cigarette."

I walked out of the room, conscious of the fact that I had left three-fourths of the food on my plate untouched.

"So very highly strung she is," I heard Gina say as I walked down the hallway. I sat alone in the living room for almost half an hour. The other guests drifted slowly in from the dining room, and Paulo followed with a bottle full of brandy. A maid soon appeared with a silver tray of snifters, and I began to relax. We sat around and chatted for a while, but it wasn't long before there was a lull in the conversation.

"Someone should tell a story," said Enrique. "Who knows a good one?"

"Let Isobel tell one," said Eduardo, strangely serious.

"Me?" I said. "I don't know any good ones."

"Then tell a bad one," said Paulo.

"I'll tell the one about the shriveled hand," I said. It was my mother's favorite. "A young man, we'll call him Ramon, was favored greatly by his father. There were only two children, the other being a girl, who was so consumed by jealousy and envy of her brother that she took to plotting against him. . . ."

The evening wore on, and everyone sat silently, under the spell of the story. All eyes were on me, transfixed, and I knew how I must have looked, with the flames flickering at the side of my face. Eduardo had heard the story, but he didn't seem to mind. He watched with the others, a sad smile on his face. Paulo watched proudly, often looking over at Eduardo and the other listeners. I reached the conclusion, which, I'm sure, had surprised no one, but still they sat back in their seats, exhausted.

"Well," said Paulo, standing up, "thank you, Isobel, for a wonderful story. I think it's time we all went to sleep."

He turned on the lights and herded everyone in the direction of the door. I found myself standing right near Eduardo.

"Good night," he said. He was very serious. I couldn't help thinking how strange he was.

"Isobel," Paulo whispered, "are you tired?" I shook my head, and he smiled.

I walked down the hall with the others, and into my room. Soon everything became quiet. I put on my nightgown and crossed the hall to Paulo's room.

6

Later that evening, I got up from the bed and walked over to the window. The house was on a mountainside, and I could see all the way down into the valley where a few lights twinkled. A fog covered the base of the mountain and I watched as it slowly crept upward.

"Must you always get up?" Paulo asked.

"I don't always," I answered, turning to look at him.

"Yes, you do. You smoke, or go to the bathroom, or look out a window." He raised his eyebrows.

"I don't know," I said.

"You want to stand up," he said. "The first to rise from a vulnerable situation. God forbid you lie, warm and safe, like other people."

"You're being absurd."

"No, I'm not," he said. "Strong. Willful. Detached. Isobel the Invincible." I put on my nightgown.

"I didn't mean for you to leave," said Paulo.

I shrugged my shoulders and opened the door. Paulo didn't protest, because I was proving his theory. I walked out into the hallway and back to my room.

I slept late the next morning. I woke at 11:30, and by the time I was dressed it was almost one. Everyone was already seated at lunch. I took my place at Paulo's right, trying to figure out the conversation. Anna wasn't listening, because they weren't talking about her. Enrique was trying to be agreeable, so I decided that something was disagreeable. Eduardo had probably thought of something that was better left unsaid, which was always a bad thing because he never kept it to himself. This was indeed the case. His cousin, Pacoy, apparently wanted to join the group in Baguio. Eduardo had made this request known to Paulo, but Paulo didn't invite him, and now Eduardo wanted to know why.

"Enrique," said Eduardo, "don't you like Pacoy?"

"Yes," said Enrique, "I think he's a delightful character."

Enrique was lying.

"I met him at a party once," Gina said.

"And you, Anna?" asked Eduardo.

"Oh yes," she said. She wasn't listening.

"And Isobel likes him."

I raised my eyebrows.

"And that's why," Eduardo continued, "I can't figure out why you didn't invite him, Paulo."

"I didn't invite him," said Paulo, "because I can't stand him. I think he's a fool."

Eduardo didn't seem shocked, although he was offended. I was offended, too, that Eduardo hadn't bothered to ask me whether I liked Pacoy or not. I looked at him narrowly.

"Pass the meat," I said.

"Isobel," said Gina, changing the subject, "we're going shopping today. I know it's rotten out, foggy and rainy, but I want to get some gifts. You will come with us, won't you?"

I glanced up at Eduardo.

"No," I said. "No, thank you. I'm sure that you will have a wonderful time, but I'm feeling very lazy. I can't picture myself doing anything but sitting in front of a fire with a book."

This met with some protest from Enrique, who, I'm sure, was sick of Eduardo's sulking, and Anna and Gina's pettiness, but I was immovable. Paulo decided to take a nap. He'd gotten up at eight to entertain people for breakfast and needed another two hours of sleep. I crawled back into bed with my cigarettes and some magazines, and stayed there until about four, when my cigarettes ran out. I walked out of the room in my socks, thinking of the silver box in the hallway, which unfortunately was host to cigars, Tabacleras, carefully wrapped in cellophane. I went to check the silver cases in the library. I found a cigarette, then took the lighter that was sitting on the table. It was a novelty lighter, and it looked like a gun. I pulled the trigger nervously.

"Last time you used a lighter like that, you set your hair on fire." I turned quickly. It was Eduardo, standing in the doorway.

"Last time I used a lighter like this, I was very drunk," I said.

"My brother's birthday."

I nodded as I inhaled from the cigarette.

"I thought you'd gone shopping with the others," I said.

"I changed my mind."

I noticed that he was wearing the shirt that had been my favorite, and started to feel uneasy. He walked over to the table and took a cigarette from the silver case.

"Can you light it for me?" he asked.

I took careful aim and pulled the trigger.

"Thank you," he said.

I nodded.

"You are very quiet, Isobel," he said.

"Well, I'm very tired. About to take a nap, you see . . ."

He put his hand on my shoulder, stopping me from leaving.

"Sit down and talk with me awhile," he said.

I sat down, trying to think of some protest.

"It's all right Isobel," he said. "I understand."

I had no idea what he was talking about.

"Paulo told me," said Eduardo, taking my hand, "how you felt about me."

I was getting nervous.

"I know what a farce it is between the two of you. I know your pride, Isobel, and how you wouldn't want to seem alone without me."

"Who told you all of this?" I asked, interrupting.

"Paulo," Eduardo answered, very seriously.

"Paulo?" I was incredulous. "Paulo told you this? Why?"

"As a favor to me," he said. "Because it's true."

"No, no. None of it. It's all a lie." I looked over to Eduardo. "I'm sorry, Eduardo. I'm sorry. I don't know why Paulo says these things."

Eduardo looked at me as he tried to recover himself.

"Then there is something going on between you and Paulo?"

"Well, of course there is." How could he have been so blind? We were quiet for some time, both stunned. He seemed to be getting angry.

"Maybe you should talk to Paulo," I said.

"Paulo. Paulo. Paulo. I am so sick of hearing about Paulo."

"He's an interesting person."

"What is so interesting about Paulo? What do you see in him? He parades you around like an object. He gives you no respect."

"He treats me better than you treated me," I said.

"That's a lie."

"Eduardo!"

"When I met you, you had nothing. Your life was empty. You had no one to love you, to talk to. I gave you substance."

"Substance? You treated me horrendously. Always dragging me around, putting me in my place."

"I expanded your mind."

"What?"

"I gave you books to read." He gestured at me with his forefinger. "New philosophies . . ."

"Ah yes," I said, "I remember that book. *The Seven Storey Mountain.* You thought that I'd read it on the outside chance that it would put meaning in my life?"

"You read it," he said.

"No, I didn't." I stared at him. "Why are you always trying to change me?"

"I feel sorry for you," he said condescendingly.

"Sorry. Right. I think you envy me because I have more friends, and much more fun." At best, this was a weak argument.

"Isobel, what makes you think that your life is so wonderful? You're nothing but everybody's whore."

This stunned me. I didn't expect to hear that from anyone, not even Eduardo. I turned and walked out of the room. My head was pounding, and I clenched my teeth.

"At least whores get paid!" I heard him scream after me.

I marched down the hallway to Paulo's room and walked in. He was sitting up in bed reading a book.

"Isobel, you look flushed," he said.

"Why did you invite him?"

"He's a friend," he said.

"Don't lie to me, Paulo. Why did you invite him?" I took his cigarette case from the dresser.

"I thought it would be amusing." He shrugged his shoulders.

"Amusing?" I said.

I turned around and left. I walked straight out of the house and onto the front lawn. The cold dampness of the grass was seeping into my socks, chilling my feet. There was a light drizzle, and fog. I lit a cigarette. The front door swung open, and I heard footsteps on the veranda.

"Isobel," Paulo called, "Isobel, come inside before you catch pneumonia. You're being absurd."

That evening we had roast pig for dinner. I was feeling more relaxed than I had felt all weekend. I looked at the empty place on the table across from me. It made me happy.

"Whatever happened to Eduardo?" asked Gina. "Did he just pack his bags and leave?"

"Yes," I said. "He can be so very high-strung."

That evening my mother called to tell me that Mando's mother had finally died. I was expected back in Manila as soon as possible. It was to be a weeklong wake, with the funeral on Sunday. The entire family would be there.

Baptisms and funerals, I thought to myself. These were the only times I got to see all the relatives. I packed my bags and had the driver load the car.

"Isobel," said Paulo, "just stay another night. It's not as if you're going to miss the funeral."

"I have to go," I said. "It's family."

Paulo raised his eyebrows, as if to dispute this.

"Enough of that," I said. "I'll see you in Manila."

And then I headed down from the cool slopes of Baguio and across the plains of Pangasinan, Tarlac, and the other provinces. Soon the skies darkened with smog and flashing lights lined the roadside. People flooded in and out of the dense traffic, and vendors competed with car horns, filling the night air with noise. We were back in Manila.

7

I hate funerals. Everyone is the same. Me, and my mother, and all Mando's sisters kneeling in the library by the coffin reciting the Rosary, decades and decades of the Rosary, and the hours passed, and early morning came. I let the beads pass through my fingers, *clack clack* as they swung against the wood. Friday, it was Sorrowful Mysteries.

"The First Sorrowful Mystery," I said, hearing my voice echo in the cold room. "The agony in the Garden. Ave Maria . . ."

I finished my part, and the others started to recite.

My eyes moved around the room, candle to candle flickering against the black wall. The coffin was surrounded by flowers, lilies and fragrant frangipani and sampaguita wreaths. And in the coffin, the thin and tired body of Maria Mercedes Rufina Reyes y Buenosantos. Her face was as smooth and waxy as the candles around her, and their flickering light gave her the illusion of life, a twitch of an eyelid, or a tightening mouth.

"The Second Sorrowful Mystery, The Scourging at the Pillar."

All heads bent in prayer, chanting, I heard our voices soft and urgent, but there was whispering, somewhere in the room, and everywhere. Voices that I could have heard if everyone had just been quiet, other souls, other times. I tried to listen and kept my voice low.

My mother knelt at my right in the pew. She pushed past me to get by once, her face streaked with tears. I looked over my shoulder to see her take off her veil and let her hair fall down on her back. She walked straight out and into the light. No one stopped reciting, even though they watched, petrified faces, hands, and hearts. I followed her out.

"Mother," I said in the kitchen, watching her fix a drink, "why are you so sad?"

"Things are getting gray," she said, "every day a darker shade. And I must sit with her in her blackness?"

"Things aren't gray," I said.

"For me, they are becoming black."

Finally it was the day of the funeral. Paulo was there, somewhere, sitting at the back with the other people from the Nueva Ecija region. I sat near the front, a chief mourner for lack of a better title. The service was endless, her many mourners, family and friends, serfs and servants, were listed along with all her good deeds, most of which she seemed to have accomplished post mortem. My mother sat in front of me, well sedated, well behaved. Nothing was natural. Even the light was filtered into purples and reds, and the air was thick with the sweet smell of incense. Children's voices floated up from the choir box, and people wept dutifully. I sat rigid, silent.

It was raining outside as we walked from the church to the cemetery. I held a new black umbrella. I thought my red one inappropriate. We gathered at the graveside. Someone read a poem, much recited, almost meaningless now. Its words bounced off the coffin like the drops of rain, no warmth in there. They lowered the casket into the ground.

"Ashes to ashes . . ." said the priest. I felt that he was addressing me.

Small children were passed over the grave, screaming, terrified, just as I had once been passed, lifted high over the pit. I remember looking down, into the grave, wondering what it would be like to lie in such eternal darkness. And then I was safe on the other side, safe from all the demons that clung to places of the dead. Evil spirits didn't dare to cross the grave. Finally, our small procession made its way back along the muddy path. I was swallowed up in a limousine, seated beside Mando's eldest sister, Serafina. She wheezed, struggling for every breath. People suspected tuberculosis, but I thought she was all rotted, every part of her, inside. Her breath was sour and her eyes yellowed. She wiped an occasional tear from her cheek, but her eyes remained cold and unemotional.

We held a small reception at our house. Modest voices, sensible conversations, but wonderful hams and roasts, sweet rolls and stewed meats, sautéed vegetables in spicy sauces, and desserts dressed in liquors and creams. Paulo was avoiding me. I knew that. He talked with his brother endlessly, and never stayed in the same place for long. I caught him at the gate as he was leaving.

"Paulo," I said.

"Isobel, how quietly you move, like a cat."

I leaned on the gate.

"You're not glad to see me," I said.

"A fighting cock is a pleasant sight in the *sabong* ring, but not at the dinner table. There's nothing pleasant or gay about this."

"I'm not a fighting cock, or a cat," I said. "I expected to hear from you. A letter, or a call."

"My father has won the party nomination. There is the planning of the ball." He stopped suddenly. "Well, let me just say, I've been very busy."

"Will you call me?" I asked.

He smiled, and turned to go to the car.

"I want you to call me," I said.

He got in the car, and I watched it drive away.

The nomination ball should have been mine. To lose Paulo one week before such an event was bad luck, and my luck was rotten. The funeral had left me in a slump, and this made everything worse. My mother was upset. She wanted to know how I'd displeased Paulo. I really didn't know. I needed someone to talk to, anyone. I knocked on Lourdes's door, just to ask her how she was, and she told me that I was "very nice between lovers." I went back into my room. I waited for Paulo to call, to say he'd changed his mind, how foolish he was, how I'd have to find a dress for the ball. The phone did ring. It was Rosita.

"Isobel," she said, "how long it's been since I've seen you."

"Shut up, Rosita. I'm not feeling well," I said.

"I've heard otherwise," she said, "and now that Paulo's found another."

I grew silent and tense.

"You do know, don't you?" I heard Rosita's voice teasing across the crackling line.

"Rosita, tell me."

"It's Antonia de Leon. Weren't you at school with her?"

I slammed the phone down. Political moves. God-damned political moves, and always me caught in the middle.

"*Bastardo, bastardo,*" I muttered to myself as I called Jorge.

"Jorge!" I said. "Are you going to the ball to-night?"

"Yes," he said.

"Take me."

"Isobel, I can't do that. I'm taking Rosario."

"Doesn't she have to do something?"

"Isobel, we were invited as a couple."

"Do you know who Paulo is taking to the ball?" I asked.

"Yes."

"Yes? And you didn't tell me?"

"Isobel, you were so depressed, and I didn't want to upset you." He was getting defensive.

"I'm upset, yes, and part of that is that I just got off the phone with Rosita."

"Rosita?"

"Jorge, get me a date. I don't care if he still has braces, or is already a grandfather. I have to go to that ball."

"Isobel, the ball is tonight."

"I know. That's why I'm in such a hurry. I'll call you later."

I hung up and ran down the hall to my mother's room.

"Mother, I have to buy a dress," I said.

"Then you're going to the ball," she said, suddenly happy.

"Yes." I turned and started walking out of the room. My mother followed close behind.

"Then he called you. I knew he would call you. I knew he would."

We walked into my room.

"Mother, he didn't call."

"I knew he liked you. How could he just forget you? How could he ever leave you?" she continued.

"Mother." I turned to look at her. "He didn't call. Paulo didn't call."

She paused. "But who are you going with?"

"I don't know."

"But how . . ."

"Jorge's finding me someone," I said.

"Oh. And you need a dress?"

"Yes. I need the most beautiful dress I can find."

"So that Paulo will notice you?" she asked.

"No, Mother."

"Then why?"

I smiled and put my hand on her shoulder.

"So that Antonia de Leon will hate me more than she's ever hated anyone in her entire life."

My mother nodded, although she didn't understand. She asked no more questions.

8

Jun Baretto. Jorge should have done better than that. Jun was Rosario's cousin, twenty-six, never had a girlfriend. He had thick glasses, was too thin, and had spent most of the past four years in Los Banos studying fish agriculture. Jorge teased me, saying, "Isobel, he's not a farmer. He's heir to the biggest fish dynasty in the Philippines." His family was very wealthy and quite powerful in his home province of Pampanga. I tried to convince myself that he really wasn't all that bad. We were in his car on the way to the Peninsula. I looked over at him. He smiled at me, big eyes, big mouth, big nostrils.

"You look like a fish," I said.

"What was that?" he asked, leaning over.

"Nothing," I said. "Nothing at all."

I learned at dinner that night that the fish we were eating had been supplied by Jun Baretto's father.

"I must say," Jun said, "it could easily be called the best fish in Luzon."

"In the Philippines," added an elderly woman sitting across from us.

"In the world," I said. Everyone nodded in agreement. This conversation was becoming more than I could bear. I got up from my seat. All the men got up, too, letting napkins fall to the ground and causing water and wine goblets to jiggle their contents onto the tablecloth.

"You must excuse me for just one moment," I said.

"Is anything the matter?" asked the woman across from me.

I shook my head, smiling at her knowingly, trying to allude to some female problem. All I really wanted was a cigarette. I walked toward the bathroom slowly, placing one foot carefully in front of the other. I heard quick footsteps and turned to see Jorge puffing behind me.

"Isobel," he said, "where were you sitting? I've been looking for you all evening."

"We are sitting over there." I pointed to the far end of the room, near the door, where our table was almost dwarfed by a box of large indoor plants. "We were talking about fish."

Jorge started laughing.

"Sorry, Isobel, but with only one day's notice, be glad you're not sitting in the kitchen. Would you like a cigarette?" He brought out a silver case.

I took one, and he lit it for me. I inhaled gratefully.

"I can't go back," I said. I gripped his arms beseechingly. "I'm so bored. If anyone says the word 'fish,' I think I'm going to die."

Jorge laughed again.

"You really should stay with him. Jun was very excited to have you as his date. In fact, he called all his friends, just to tell them about it."

"Marvelous," I said. "Now the whole of Manila knows that I went to the nomination ball with Jun the Fish Prince."

"Isobel, just have fun. That's why we're here, isn't it?"

I raised an eyebrow.

"What are you planning?" He seemed a little worried. "A scene is not going to be good for either of you."

"I have nothing planned, Jorge. I don't exactly know why I'm here, but I assure you, it's not to have a good time, which is good, because I'm not."

"I must return to my table," he said. "You should, too."

I nodded.

"In a little while," I said, "when I finish this." I raised my cigarette.

He nodded, although still unsure of me, and went back to his table. I finished the cigarette and walked slowly back to mine.

Later, I found myself standing with Jun in the room with the bar and jazz ensemble. I spotted Paulo standing with Antonia and some other people at the far end of the room.

"Jun," I said, "I've just seen a girlfriend that I wish to have a private word with. I'll meet you where the dancing is." I didn't even bother to sound convincing. He didn't seem to notice.

"Are you sure?" he asked.

"Yes," I said. I looked at him, irritated. He was such an absurd person.

He left, and I stood at the edge of the room, watching Paulo closely, peering through the merry groups and smoke. I saw him pat a man on the back and raise his empty glass. He was going to the bar. I raced across the room and positioned myself at the punch bowl, my back turned in his direction. He came and stood right near me. I could smell his cologne.

"Big green thing with a parasol," he said.

I turned.

"Double vodka tonic," I ordered the *barrista*. "Hello, Paulo."

Paulo seemed surprised to see me, but kept calm. I could see that I was making him nervous.

"You should try changing your drink," he said.

"All right," I said. "Something red and fruity. No parasol, please."

We both got our drinks and turned to face each other. I looked at the whiteness of his shirt over the rim of my glass. He addressed me nervously.

"Isobel, don't do anything rash. It wouldn't look any better for you than it would for me." He looked up and around the room, smiling stiffly.

"You're appealing to my intellect," I said.

He nodded, feeling more confident. I took my drink and threw it all over the front of his shirt. It looked like he'd been shot. I walked quickly to the door, pushing through groups of people who stared at me in awe.

"No need to be embarrassed," I heard Paulo say loudly. "We all spill things every now and then."

Jorge grabbed my arm as I walked out of the room.

"Isobel, what on earth is going on?"

"He should have let me order vodka," I said. I walked quickly through the lobby, bumping into people, offering no apologies. I let my hair fall around my shoulders and took off my gloves, twirling them around as I made my way to the door. A taxi was waiting out front.

"Excuse me," I said, addressing a blond gentleman in an ill-fitting Hawaiian shirt, and a pretty young prostitute who were about to get in. I gave the cab-driver my address, then sat back in the seat, waiting for myself to cry, or get angry or agitated, for some feeling of regret to come over me. But nothing did happen. I sat there in some state of frozen time, and remained like that until I reached the house.

9

Mother was up when I got home that night.

"What happened?" she asked. I was glad that she didn't seem too hopeful.

"Nothing much," I lied. She could hear it from someone else.

She was glaring at me when I sat down for dinner the next day. Lourdes and Mando were there. It wasn't often that the four of us sat down together.

"What are you doing tonight?" my mother asked.

"Nothing."

"Nothing? Or do you just not want to tell me?"

I was silent.

"Aren't you going to eat? You're already too thin."

"Pass the rice," I said.

"You have to talk to the maid," said Mando. "She's putting too much starch in my shirts again."

He had food in his mouth. I could see every grain of rice.

"Why don't you tell the maid?" I asked.

He looked up at me.

"What?"

"Why don't you tell the maid yourself?" I repeated.

"I never see her," he said. He was annoyed. He looked across at me.

"Auring!" I screamed. "Auring, *halika dito. Bilis!*"

Mando looked down at his food, and started eating. Auring came running, bewildered.

"Ma'am?" she said.

"Señorito has something to say to you."

"I have nothing to say," said Mando.

"Tell her what you wanted to say," I insisted.

He looked up at the maid, who fidgeted nervously.

"Get out," he said. "Go back to the kitchen."

Auring left, confused. I sat in my seat, staring down at my food, aware that Lourdes was looking at me triumphantly.

"I'll tell her tomorrow, Mando," my mother said.

I pushed my chair back from the table. "I'm going to my room," I said.

"Aren't you going out tonight?" my mother asked.

"No, Mother. I'm not going out."

I stood up and walked out of the room.

"You talk to that daughter of yours," I heard Mando say as I walked through the *sala*. Mando was my mother's heaviest cross, but he thought that I was.

When I woke up the following Saturday morning, it felt like it was ten o'clock. I had been lying in bed for over an hour. Everything had been thought and rethought over the course of the last week, and I was bored with seeing no one but Lourdes and my mother, who was growing nervous about my constant presence around the house. I got up and turned off the air conditioner. Everything was suddenly quiet, as if someone had blocked my ears. I pulled the curtain back, just a little to see into the yard. Auring was feeding the dogs. She called out each of their names, Pilot, Simon, Tyro, and they came running, barking loudly, leaping at the food and devouring it, until there was nothing left in the bowl. I stepped back from the window. There was a knock at the door. It was Doris, carrying the phone.

"Ma'am, it's for you, ma'am," she said. "Please don't hang up."

I took the phone. It had to be Jorge.

"Hello," I said softly.

"Isobel, don't hang up."

It was Jorge. "Why should I?"

"That's a good question, but you've been hanging up all week, and I'm somewhat accustomed to it."

I remained silent.

"Well, what is the matter? What did I do?"

"It isn't what you did, Jorge, it's what everyone did, every last person, and I'm still mad."

"If anyone should be mad, Isobel, it's me. I went through the trouble of finding you a date, whom you leave most unceremoniously. Not only that, but you insult the host in a very embarrassing way. If anyone deserves an apology, it's me."

"But Jorge, it isn't that simple."

"All right. It's not that simple." He was unsympathetic.

There was a brief silence.

"Isobel, what are you doing tonight?"

"I'm free, Jorge, hopelessly free, and bored."

"Good," he said. "Monching's having a party. He'd be crushed if you didn't go. He's had me calling you all week."

"He wants a firsthand account of just what happened at the nomination ball."

"He wants to see you," said Jorge.

"I'm glad he wants to see me, for whatever reason," I said. "Can you pick me up?"

"Of course. Ten?"

Ten was fine. Nine would have been fine. Even eight. I needed to get out.

. . .

We arrived at the Polo Club, where Monching had decided to throw his party. I told Jorge to go ahead while I stopped off at the powder room. The drive had been congested with cars and people, and every walkway, including the one to the bathroom, seemed to be full of people, many of whom were a little loud, a little unsteady, and very drunk. I wondered what potent drink Monching was serving. I started walking to the main room, trying to figure out who recognized me, who was glad that I was back. I looked for Paulo. I knew he was there somewhere, with Antonia. I would surprise him tonight. I would surprise everyone, because tonight I didn't care about him, or Antonia. Tonight the only one that mattered was me. I spotted Jorge talking to Monching and some others, Baby Matenzano, Arturo Cruz, near the bar, and went over to join them. Jorge was telling a story.

"And then she takes her drink, something with a lot of grenadine in it, and throws it all over him."

I'm sure that everyone had heard the story a dozen times, but still they managed to look surprised and laughed as if it was the first.

I put my hand on Jorge's shoulder.

"Were you just talking about me?" I asked.

"As a matter of fact," said Jorge, "we were."

"Isobel," said Monching. "how beautiful you look."

I rolled my eyes upward and leaned on Jorge.

"Getting tired of it?" asked Baby.

"No, not really." I smiled.

"I want to walk around the party," said Monching, "just to make sure everyone's having fun. And I'm taking Isobel with me." He offered his plump arm.

"Well," he said when we had reached the terrace, "I want to hear your version of the incident with Paulo."

"It wasn't really an incident," I said, smiling. "It was an accident."

"Oh really?"

"Yes. Yes, you see, I wasn't going to go to the ball at all, but then Jorge called saying that Jun Baretto was just dying to go to the ball with me, so finally, after much pleading, I agreed."

"How very generous you are, Isobel."

"Yes, I know. Anyway, I spent the whole evening avoiding Paulo."

Monching was laughing.

"I was," I said. "I went to get a drink at the bar, and didn't notice that Paulo was standing right next to me."

"You must have been surprised," said Monching.

"Oh yes," I said, "so surprised, in fact, that I spilled my drink down the front of his shirt."

"I like Jorge's version better," he said.

"So do I."

We laughed.

"Have you seen Eduardo around?" asked Monching.

"No. Is he here?"

"Him, and his new girlfriend."

"His new girlfriend? Good for him," I said. "What's she like?"

"She grew up in the States," he said, and then in a softer voice, "She thinks she's American."

"Are they fond of each other?"

"Of each other, I'm not sure; of themselves, very."

I laughed.

"Are they very impressive?"

"Eduardo has his books, and she has her accent, but no, I'm not impressed."

"Monching, does anything impress you?"

He stopped walking and looked at me.

"You impress me, Isobel."

"Me, Monching? How absurd. Why?"

"Because you're like, *makahiya*."

"Monching, that's a weed. It grows everywhere."

"But Isobel, there is something very special about the *makahiya*. If you step on it, it collapses, crumples up, looks like it's dead, but if you watch, it slowly starts to stand again. Soon, it looks like it did before you stepped on it."

"And I'm like that?"

"Yes. Very much so."

"I'd rather be something with thorns which didn't allow people to step on me in the first place."

Monching laughed.

"Maybe we need drinks," he said.

"I can see how drunk most people are, and it isn't even midnight. What have you been giving us?"

Monching signaled for a waiter, who came over with a tray laden with purplish drinks.

"Nothing I wouldn't drink myself," he said. He handed me a drink and took one for himself. I looked at him over my rim suspiciously, then took a sip.

"Drink up!" he said. He patted the bottom of my glass. I watched him take two more gulps and drain the glass, tilting his head back and letting the last few drops fall into his mouth.

"Come on, Isobel," he said. "I want to make sure you have fun."

I drank about one-third, which seemed to satisfy him.

"We're off to the dance floor," he said. For someone so large, Monching moved very quickly. I followed his purple silk shirt as it bobbed between the groups and drifted toward the dance floor, a large purple beacon in a sea of evening black. The drink was beginning to go to my head. There seemed to be clouds moving across the room, sudden spots of fog in my vision. I looked to see just how much I'd had to drink and realized that I'd finished the whole drink. I set the glass on a table and trotted a little unsteadily after Monching, who always seemed to be a few steps ahead of me. I found myself in the middle of the dance floor walking into people, looking for Monching. Finally, I spotted him dancing with a girl in the middle of the floor. People had cleared a little space for them, and Monching swung his rolling hips and flicked his little dance partner out in a series of spins and dips. I was standing beside a young man, who was also alone, in the middle of the dance floor, for no apparent reason. He noticed me looking at him.

"My date," he said, pointing at Monching's dance partner.

"His party," I answered. "But don't worry. He prefers men."

We watched them for a while. The girl reminded me of a planet moving in orbit around Monching, the sun.

"I think Monching makes a very good sun," I said.

"Yes, he does," said the young man, who I'm sure had no idea what I was talking about.

"Would you like a drink?" he said.

"Well, yes, I would," I said.

There was a line at the bar, so I left him waiting there and went off to the powder room. Coming out of a stall, I saw Antonia de Leon fixing her hair in the mirror. She saw me and froze, then continued smoothing her hair back in quick, agitated motions.

"Antonia," I said, "do you remember that Ping-Pong tournament sophomore year?"

"Yes," she said.

"I won." I walked out of the bathroom, realizing how very dull my mind was. Paulo was out there, standing by a large plant.

"Isobel," he said, smiling, "it came out." He pointed at his shirt.

"What a shame," I said. He was standing in a cloud, and I couldn't make out his features.

"What have you been doing lately?" he asked. He wanted to know if I was seeing anyone.

"I've been busy," I said.

The door to the bathroom opened, and Antonia peered out. I turned to Paulo.

"Does she melt in your arms?" I asked. "Does she call you 'darling'?" I started laughing, amused with my joke, and went off to find the little man with my drink.

"She's drunk," I heard Paulo tell Antonia.

The clouds seemed to be lifting. I was very glad to get another drink.

"I can't find my date," said the young man. "Why don't we dance?"

I moved onto the dance floor, trying not to spill my drink. All of a sudden, Monching appeared behind my dance partner and started making obscene gestures at him. I started laughing.

"What's the matter?" he asked.

"Nothing, it's just that Monching approves of you."

He spun around, but Monching had bounced off.

I spotted him on the far side of the room. He was jumping up and down, waving at me, calling my attention to the fact that Jorge was in the process of picking up a girl who looked like she was sixteen. I started laughing again.

"I think Monching makes a very good Pan," I said.

"Yes, he does," said the man.

The clouds were back. The evening drifted somewhat aimlessly over conversations and renewed acquaintances, drinks, and cigarettes. At around two A.M., I found myself standing with my man friend by the bar. Monching was bouncing over, singing along with the music from the dance floor.

"Isobel," said Monching, smoothing his mustache, looking at me out of the corner of his eye. "Who is your handsome friend?"

"I have no idea," I said.

Monching was appalled.

"Then you haven't been introduced?"

"No. We met by accident on the dance floor. You took his date."

"I'm sorry," said Monching.

"Don't be. She was nowhere so entertaining as Isobel," he said, turning to me.

"Who are you?" I said. I was bothered by the fact that he knew who I was.

"Frankie, Aguilar."

"No relation?" I asked.

"Paulo's cousin."

"Oh, my God," I said, lighting a cigarette. "That's hilarious."

"You're not laughing," he said.

"Inside, I'm laughing."

Monching was amused.

"Get me a drink," he said, gesturing at us.

"I'll get it," I said. I walked straight to the bar and noticed a familiar figure, slouched at one end. It was Paulo.

"Where's Antonia?" I said.

"She's in the bathroom." His speech was slurred.

"She goes there a lot, doesn't she?"

He turned to face me, knocking several drinks off the bar in the process. We had everyone's attention. Paulo was angry.

"You know," he said loudly, to the crowd more than to me, "we're taking bets in the men's room. We're guessing who your next man will be."

"Oh really," I heard myself say.

I scanned the room, where people were lined up around us, as if we were at a cockfight. I noticed Antonia standing at the edge of the people. She looked on the verge of tears. I turned to her.

"I think he's going to need help," I said. "Why don't you help him?"

People parted, leaving a clear path of exit for me.

"I'm so sorry, Isobel," said Monching.

"So am I. I forgot your drink."

"Isobel, I didn't know that Paulo was going to be such an ass," he said.

"Who did you bet on, Monching?" I asked.

"What?"

I laughed.

"Who did you bet on, in the men's room?" I asked again.

Frankie smiled.

"I bet on me," he said.

We all laughed. I linked my left arm through Monching's, and my right arm through Frankie's. We went off to find Jorge and tell him the story. But Jorge had left with a young girl an hour before, someone said. And somewhere, in the party, we heard there was a man looking for his little sister.

10

No lights were on in the house at four A.M. None but my mother's cigarette, a little red glow in the blackness of the dining room. I closed the door behind me.

"Frankie Aguilar. A play on Thursday. Private box. Drinks afterward. He offered dinner, but I declined," I said.

"Isobel," my mother said, "don't be like that. Come talk to me."

I walked toward her in the darkness, unsure of the furniture, feeling for the frame of the archway. I stepped off the marble onto carpet and caught the smell of cigarette smoke. Her face was barely lit by the glow, and she looked tired, worn.

"I'm going to sleep now." I kissed her forehead. "Why don't you come up?"

"I like this," she said. "I like this blackness."

I went upstairs, and prepared for bed.

I talked to Jorge the following afternoon.

"Isobel, I'll pick you up at eight, bring you to the play, but then I have to leave."

"Where are you going?" I asked.

"Nowhere really. Out with the guys."

"Guys?"

"Friends from college. People you don't know."

"Jorge, you're not doing anything stupid, are you?"

"I'm going out with my friends."

"I'm your friends," I said. "What is it? Can't you talk about it?"

"Not right now," he said.

I imagined him scratching his head.

"Later?" I pressed.

"Yes, all right," he said.

"Eight," I said. "Don't be late. Remember last time you were late. It ruined a good part of my evening."

• • •

His car pulled up in front of the house at 8:15. I trotted down the stairs and ran out the door to meet him.

"Isobel, I'm not late, am I?"

I shook my head.

"What were you talking about on the phone?" I asked.

"On the phone?"

"Yes," I said, impatient.

"Isobel . . ."

"It's that girl from the party, isn't it? It's that girl!"

"No, no," he said.

"Yes, it is. Jorge, she's half your age!"

"She is not," he said, then catching himself, "You're being absurd."

We got into the car.

"Jorge, you better tell me, or I'll start imagining things, and what I imagine is bound to be far worse than anything you could do."

"We're going out for dinner tonight."

"And . . ."

He smiled, and I started to laugh.

"There's nothing to tell," he said, somewhat guarded. "I'll tell you afterward. She's really not that young."

"How old is she?"

"She doesn't act her age."

"I appreciate the fact that you've stopped trying to lie to me."

"And I appreciate the fact that—" He stopped short and started gesturing with his hands.

"The fact that I haven't mentioned Rosario?"

"Yes," he said, and he started to laugh.

"You're a bad man, Jorge," I said.

"Isobel, I thought you were going to help me rationalize this."

For some reason, I was gleeful. I was almost proud of him. His new romance excited me more than anything I had done recently, and I pinched his arm and urged him on with my laughter. Jorge seemed surprised and relieved at my reaction. He thought of new, funny things to say, indulging himself in my lack of conscience. It reminded me of when he had first met Rosario, young, sweet, innocent, and what I'd had to say about her. I told him that if one could not look after herself, it was hardly another person's fault. Unfortunately, not everyone felt the same way. Or even if they did, it seemed only to apply to me.

We arrived at the Cultural Center on time. The play was not as well attended as the ballet. I knew absolutely nothing about it. I asked Jorge what the name of the play was.

"*Mirandola.* It stars Amy Puno."

"Amy Puno? President's daughter Amy Puno?"

Jorge nodded.

"Can she act?"

"I don't think so. Does it matter?" he asked.

I shook my head.

We went in and saw Frankie standing with some friends at the foot of the stairs. He was wearing a baggy suit, very fashionable. His hair was carefully slicked back.

"Jorge, I'm bored already," I said.

"Sorry, Isobel. This is when I leave."

"How could you leave me for another woman?" I said, half-serious. I patted his arm. Frankie walked over when he saw us.

"Hello, Jorge," he said.

I looked over at Frankie. He smiled at me, and suddenly I felt depressed. It was just another man, as Paulo had said there would be, another man at the Cultural Center.

"Is anything the matter?" he said.

"No, no. I was just dizzy for a second. Maybe we should go to the box." I was finding it hard to be enthusiastic. I smiled, but it was forced. I felt drained. I could hardly walk.

"Our box," he said, letting me choose a seat in the Aguilar family box. I had a familiar view of a familiar scene. Actors came onto the stage, but they didn't dance. They walked in, dragging their feet with no music, and a harsh, all-encompassing light. I could recognize most of the actors through the garish makeup and powdered wigs. They clustered in little groups around the stage, gesturing, reciting, speaking Filipino with English accents. That was supposed to be the gimmick of the play, but it sounded more like the squawking of chickens than anything else. Then, from the right wing, Amy Puno walked out to center stage. She seemed more a Victorian nightmare than a vision of beauty. Well stuffed into a shiny satin bodice, she brought to mind a ripe fruit, ready to burst. Her hair had somehow been persuaded to stay in a series of sausagelike curls, which bounced off her cheeks and around her face in much the same manner in which she bounced across the stage. The actors flocked around her billowing skirts, and she dismissed their advances with well-calculated flicks of a lace fan. I looked over at Frankie, half expecting to see the side of Paulo's face, but he was just another man sitting in the same place. At first I longed for the play to be over, but then I realized that things were probably going to be worse afterward. Frankie asked me some questions during the play, if I was cold, how I liked it. I always managed a courteous response. I smiled. The play wore on. I had no idea of what was happening, and no interest in the characters. When intermission came, I was greatly relieved to see that Frankie had fallen asleep. I passed him quietly, careful not to wake him, and walked out to the lobby, almost blinded by my depression. There were twin staircases leading down to the main foyer. I stopped at the balcony, watching all the people, women in jewellike dresses, and men in suits and embroidered shirts, swarming like ants beneath me, and up and down the staircase in a steady stream. I stayed lost in thought, imagining myself somewhere down there, pushing through the people with a lit cigarette and a drink. It was as if I could picture myself, white dress, hair pulled back, same gold necklace, standing and conversing artfully. There would be a little man for me to hold on to and to get me a little drink. Somewhere in Manila, Paulo and Antonia were making each other's life miserable, and here I was, miserable alone.

"I don't know why I came over. You don't look like you need company, and I don't like many people, but I felt compelled to come over."

I turned to see a thin, pale, Spanish mestizo. He held a short cigarette between his long slender fingers, and he gestured at me with this hand. I stared at him.

"You're Isobel della Fortuna, aren't you?"

"What?"

"Miss della Fortuna, I saw you throw a drink on Paulo Aguilar."

I sank even further.

"That's why I came," he said, "because misery enjoys company, and you are truly miserable."

"I think you should leave, whoever you are."

I turned to look at him, but he was no longer there. Granted, there were a good many places for him to go, but I couldn't help feeling that I'd been visited by an apparition. Intermission ended, and people filed back to their boxes. I followed.

Frankie was awake.

"Was I long?" I asked.

"No, not really," he said. The lights dimmed, and I settled back into my melancholy. Players came out from the wings, and my mind wandered again. I thought of the strange, thin man in the lobby. Maybe everyone thought of me that way, as a most recent incident, or even worse, as a present lover. Down on stage, Amy Puno had broken into song. She had chosen her one perfect love from her bevy of suitors, and they were to be united forever more. I cringed. Finally, the performance came to a close. I decided that drinks were a good idea. I told Frankie that I had to be home at one. My mother had plans for the following morning. I don't know whether he bought this or not. I didn't bother to notice.

We walked out to the drive, waiting for the car. I looked down toward the bay. Standing over to my left was the strange man, the apparition. I watched him light a cigarette, alone, unaware of me.

"Frankie, who is that?" I asked.

"Gregorio del Pilar."

"Do you know him?"

"Me, no. But he's mad you know, violent."

"He doesn't look violent," I said.

"All the sane people look crazy, and all the crazy people look sane."

A car pulled up beside him. He put out his cigarette and got in.

"Isobel," said Frankie, calling my attention to the fact that the car had arrived.

"I wonder if he does the same things that we do," I said.

"Who?"

"Gregorio del Pilar."

"Why?"

I shrugged my shoulders. I had no answer.

11

The next day I had to meet Frankie at the Peninsula for a late lunch. I really wasn't in the mood for that, or for anything, but I didn't know what else I was supposed to do. I put on a suit, houndstooth, and black shoes, brushed my hair back. I looked like a businessman, as most of the Friday lunch crowd at the Pen were. And here I was, not a lawyer, or a banker, or a politician, but "someone who goes to lunch," a profession of sorts. I purposely arrived half an hour early, in order to get a few drinks, even though my senses already felt numbed. I was depressed, but I tried to think of witty things to say about the previous evening.

"Did you see Marietta?" I rehearsed to myself. "Such a beautiful tiara, and such an ugly face."

It sounded flat to me, even then, when usually I imagined light laughter, and comments that would be annexed to what I had just said. I was shown to a table near the string quartet.

"Violin. Cello," I said absentmindedly. The violinist began a faster melody, swiftly soaring upward. I started to hum along, my eyes focused on the instrument. I knew the piece, but couldn't remember what it was called. As I pondered this, watching the violinist madly sawing away, I realized I was crying. Large, slow drops rolled down my cheeks and, uneventfully, onto the table. I didn't move or try to wipe them away. I sat, frozen, my eyes fixed on the violin, humming in time with soft, even tones. The piece slowed. A sad melody was soon picked up by the other players. Nothing entered my mind. I could see the waiters and waitresses gathering at the edge of the room, watching me, unsure of what to do. I didn't really care. At that moment, I was perfectly content to sit, immobile, for the rest of my life, letting my tears roll onto the tabletop. Perhaps I was sitting there for five minutes, maybe longer, before he placed the handkerchief on the table. At first I ignored it, along with the rest of the room, but then he took my hand and placed the handkerchief inside it. I blinked to clear two large tears out of my eyes. It was Gregorio del Pilar.

"Please leave me," I said.

"You may cry if you wish, but not alone, and certainly not here." I stared at him. He was wearing a suit, too broad for his narrow shoulders, and a white shirt. He had a sad air about him, like someone who spent time with the dead or was accustomed to misery. It was comforting.

"I'll bring you home," he said.

Without a second thought, I got into the back of his car. I would have gone anywhere with anyone.

"Where do you live?" he asked.

"New Manila, but please don't take me there." I was still crying, but now had the presence of mind to wipe off an occasional tear with the back of my hand.

"Where would you like to go?" he asked.

I shrugged my shoulders.

"I live in Antipolo. It's far, but quiet."

"Whatever," I whispered.

"*Sa bahay*," he said, addressing the driver, and then to me: "You were meeting someone?"

I nodded.

"The man you were with last night?"

"Yes."

"Is this something that should be discussed with him?"

I looked at him, incredulous, and then started laughing, almost coughing.

"I'm afraid I don't understand," he said.

"Do you know who I am?"

"Yes, of course," he answered.

"Well, then you know that it might have something to do with him—Frankie? Is that his name?" I stared at him. Gregorio put up his hands in a gesture of total bewilderment. "It also might have something to do with Paulo, Eduardo, Marco, Alexi, or Francis." I looked at him accusingly.

"I don't know," he said, pausing between each word. I rested my face in my hands.

"What do you want from me?" I asked, my voice muffled.

"I don't know. Nothing?"

"Nothing?" I was trying desperately to offend him.

"Nothing." He nodded, more sure of himself.

When we arrived at his house, my crying had degenerated into a general puffiness, pounding headache, and sniffles. I placed my cool hands around my face, trying to take away the feverish feeling. Worse than that was the knowlege that I had probably made myself very ugly. I felt insecure.

The main house was magnificent, a great, symmetrical classical house of polished white and green tile.

"No, not there." He led me aside to a smaller house, brick, enshrouded by trees and covered in ivy.

"Do you live here alone?" I asked.

"Yes. My grandmother used to live here, but she died a few years ago. Now it's just me. My parents live in the big house." He paused on the pathway and held my arm. "Look up there." He pointed toward a large mango tree. Sitting high in the branches was a magnificent gibbon. There was a leather band about his waist, which fixed him to a chain.

"He's beautiful. Is he yours?" I asked.

"Well, I suppose he is, but I prefer to think of him as a noble captive."

The gibbon looked down on us disdainfully, like a silver-white deity, through the leaves. Suddenly, with a loud screech, he leaped from his perch with incredible speed. He was coming straight for me. I stood, frozen in my place, hearing the breaking of branches and my pounding heart, but just when he was almost upon us, his chain ran out. Jerked back powerfully, he was forced to seat himself on the low branches of a banana tree, a mere five feet from where we stood. I breathed a sigh of relief.

"I suppose you're going to tell me that I shouldn't have been scared."

"No," he said. "That gibbon could probably have torn us apart." Then he smiled. It was the first time I'd seen him smile. There was something eerie about it, disturbing. As I'd previously observed, he was far more suited to misery than happiness. When he smiled, it was as if his face had been confused into a series of unfamiliar wrinkles, but his eyes held something new, a twinkle unfamiliar and strange.

We entered the house through a large, broad door, which led into a small hallway. There was a magnificent stairway that encompassed the entire vestibule. It was carved out of mahogany, broad shallow planks supported by ornate banisters, and runners decorated with leaves and flowers that twisted up the sides, ready to give new growth in unexpected directions. It ascended in a low incline, as old staircases tend to do, and terminated abruptly into a mirror on the second floor.

"This is a very impressive staircase," I said. "When was the house built?"

"About twenty years ago," he said. "But all the doors, window frames, and the staircase came from my grandmother's house in the province, in Laguna. That house was built in 1875. When my grandmother moved here, the provincial house was in a state of total disrepair. This was all we could salvage."

He extended his hand in an invitation to go upstairs.

"I want to show you the windows," he said. I walked up the stairs, which creaked quietly beneath my feet. I saw my reflection in the mirror, my face swollen and red, and Gregorio's behind me, his hollow cheeks and large, silent, eyes. We paused at the top of the stairs. Gregorio's eyes skirted around the room, as if he was looking for someone. Finally, he addressed me.

"This is where I live. Welcome."

The room was just a wide hall, barely accommodating the stairs. At the far end, across from the mirror, were the most wonderful *capiz* windows. A grid of dark wood held the small shell panes in place. The entire window glowed like alabaster, as light persistently pushed through. The room was dim in the muted light.

"Is it always this dark?" I asked.

"You can slide the windows back," he said, "but I like it this way." He opened a door to his left. "My study."

The room was small, with the same *capiz* windows and strange light. There was a large, ornately carved desk against one wall. The leather-bound books that sat on the surface were meticulously arranged. Pencils, pens, and paper clips sat neatly in their corresponding containers. Even the letter opener had been placed at a right angle to the edge of the desk. Above the desk hung a portrait of a Spaniard with a long, curling mustache, who was in full military regalia.

"Your grandfather?" I asked. He nodded.

Shelves lined most of the other walls from floor to ceiling, except on the wall by the door, where a cupboard stood. The doors were closed shut, and a large key rested in the lock.

"May I?" I said, walking to a shelf.

"Of course," he said.

I took an untitled leather-bound book off the shelf. It was a stamp album.

"Is the entire shelf stamps?" I asked,

"The drawers at the bottom contain coins. I am a great collector."

"Stamps, coins . . ." I said, running my hands along the shelves. I pulled out a box. "Soldiers?"

"Yes. They're tin. I paint them myself. What you have there is the Persian cavalry, Cyrus, you know."

I didn't know. I turned to him.

"What else do you collect?"

"The usual. Spoons, model cars, war bonds, Oriental snuff bottles."

"Oriental snuff bottles?"

"That collection would probably appeal to you more than the rest." He took a leather case off the shelf and opened it. It was lined with red velvet, which cradled half a dozen bottles of different sizes, three to four inches tall. Each bottle had its place, as each was a different shape, and the case had been made specially to house them. He picked out one of carved ivory, which depicted an old sage going up a steep path on a donkey.

"It's beautiful," I said.

"Would you like to hold it?" He offered me the bottle. I took it, my hand briefly touching his, which was ice cold, then quickly handed it back. He put the bottle back in its niche and set the case on the shelf.

"What's in there?" I said, pointing at the cupboard.

"A scientific interest. I don't think it would be of much interest to you." I noticed an odd glimmer in his eye. "You're welcome to look. Turn the key to the left."

I fumbled with the lock until the key turned with a click, and I slowly opened the cabinet.

It took me a minute to understand what I was seeing.

"You collect babies?" I whispered.

"Not babies," he corrected me, "fetuses. And I don't collect them. They represent various weeks and months of the gestation cycle. Two months." He pointed at the tadpole. "And seven months." He pointed at the tight-fisted baby whose mouth was forever open in a silent scream.

"Babies in jars." I turned to him. "Where do you get them from?"

"Oh, hospitals, clinics. There's a rhesus monkey on the bottom shelf, if you'd like to compare."

"No," I said. "That's quite all right." I closed the doors and turned the key to the right. "Anything else?"

"Rare books"—he shrugged his shoulders—"knives."

I realized where I was. Frankie's voice was suddenly screaming in my head.

Insane! Violent!

I took two steps back. No one knew I was there.

No one knew who I was with, except maybe the waiters. Had they seen us leave together? And the other house was so far. If I screamed, no one could hear me, and if they did, they would think it was the gibbon. I felt the blood drain from my face.

"Isobel, you're so pale. Is everything all right?"

"It's nothing," I lied. "It's just that I should be going home."

"You're scared, aren't you? Scared of me."

"No, of course not," I said.

"No need to be apologetic. It's quite understandable. I know what other people say."

"I don't know what you're talking about," I said, unconvincingly.

"Just like people," he said, ignoring me. "Label you, never tell the full story, never give you a chance to explain yourself." He was becoming agitated. It was making me nervous.

"Would you like to talk about it?" I immediately regretted saying this, because it sounded so trite, but he hadn't heard me.

"What?"

"I haven't heard that much about you," I said.

"They say I'm crazy," he informed me.

"Of course not." I seemed to be saying that over and over.

"Do you know why they say that?"

I shook my head. I wanted to leave. He was dragging me out of my hell, and into his.

"I had a brother who died when he was nine," he began. "It was an accident, with a gun. It went off suddenly. We didn't know it was loaded. He died instantly." He was suddenly tired. He looked around for a place to sit. I remained standing, leaning against the windowsill.

"Lots of people have dead brothers," I said. "It doesn't mean you're crazy."

He looked at me. "I was holding the gun when it went off. They say I shot him."

"That's ridiculous," I said, trying to sound casual.

"Not that ridiculous. I was very jealous of him, but not that jealous." He was looking up at me with pleading eyes, as if he himself were unsure. "He was my older brother. I idolized him. I would never kill him."

I shook my head vigorously in agreement. We were silent for a time. He sat in the red leather chair behind his desk, tormented, grieving. Finally he rested his head on the desk. I watched him silently.

"Isobel, I'm so very sorry, but I'll have to ask you to go home with the driver."

"That's quite all right," I said. "Thank you for everything." He made no effort to respond. I tiptoed quietly across the floorboards and down the staircase, shutting the door quietly behind me. I walked down the path, and my mind ran through all the day's events. Then I turned, just to take one last look at the little brick house. Gregorio was watching me. He had pulled one of the *capiz* shutters aside and peered out, thin and pale, alone, down through the leaves.

12

"Isobel, telephone." My mother was knocking on my door.

"I'm in the shower," I said. She walked in.

"You are not," she retorted. Auring was standing behind her, carrying the telephone, like an offering. "He's called twice this morning."

I walked over to the phone and lifted the receiver.

"Hello?" I hoped it was Jorge.

"Isobel, it's Frankie. I've been trying to get you all morning."

"Really? I've been here." My mother listened intently beside me.

"What happened to you yesterday? I waited at the hotel for over an hour."

"I was there, but I got sick. I had to go home."

"I called your house. They said you weren't there."

"That's because I was at my uncle's house. It's nearer to the Pen." Bringing up the subject of my "uncle" always cut discussions short.

"Well, how about dinner tonight? I was thinking of going to the Champagne Room, Manila Hotel."

"The Champagne Room." I spoke out loud, a big mistake. My mother looked at me, eyebrows raised expectantly. Auring looked from my mother to me and back again. Auring was getting nervous.

"Tonight," I said. "Well, of course I can. I'd love to."

"I'll pick you up at 8:30."

"Wonderful." I hung up the phone.

"Isobel, you didn't say good-bye," Mother said. I ignored her. "Where did you go yesterday? You weren't here until six."

"It's unimportant," I said.

"But . . ."

"It's unimportant."

Mother looked directly at me and realized that she wasn't going to find out. She turned to leave, Auring following with the telephone. I stepped back, feeling behind me for the bedpost. It was going to be another nightmare evening.

Frankie's arrival at the house, the drive to the hotel, our being seated, is blurred. I was preoccupied thinking about Gregorio, in fact. I imagined him walking over to the closet and turning the key, shaking the jar with the baby in it, and watching it bob slowly up and down. I then imagined him sitting at his desk and lighting a cigarette, tapping it carefully so as not to let any ashes fall on the desktop. And then I thought of him sitting, with his face in his hands, staring blankly across the room, thinking of the past and the narrow future, to be spent in dark rooms, thumbing through the pages of leather-bound books. I felt sorry for him, as I'm sure he felt for me.

Our table was in a good location, not too near the kitchen, or the entrance. It was one of those "tables for two," with a stiff white linen tablecloth, and flower vase with a single rosebud and sprig of fern. The waitress brought us menus. Frankie immediately became engrossed in his. I, however, could not focus on anything. My eyes were looking straight at the menu, but it meant nothing to me. I decided that I should probably just order whatever Frankie ordered. That was usually safe.

Frankie had crossed his legs out to the side of the table. His cigarette was elegantly poised between his fingers. He kept tossing his long straight bangs out of his face by jerking his head back. Then he tilted his head far to the right, almost at a forty-five-degree angle to his neck, which kept the bangs out of his eyes. In this unnatural position, he continued to study the menu.

"The steak is really the specialty here, but I think I'll try something different," he said.

I stared at him blankly.

"Maybe the *cingiale alla cacciatore*. It's roasted boar meat covered with a tomato sauce flavored with Italian herbs and spices."

I didn't know what he was talking about.

"Maybe I should adhere to the French cuisine and order escargots. It's a butter sauce that they serve it with here. I've had it before, and it's excellent." He paused to look at me.

"But then again"—he raised his cigarette and gestured in circular motions—"filet mignon is a steak, and probably would be remarkably like the French original."

"I really don't care," I said.

"What was that?" He seemed a little surprised.

I stood up. "I said I really don't care whether you order the *cingiale* with herb butter or the steak with tomatoes. You can order whatever you want. It doesn't make any difference to me. I don't care."

"Isobel, you're not making another one of those scenes, are you?"

I tossed my napkin onto the table.

"If you leave now, it's definitely the last time I ask you out to eat, anywhere." He seemed peeved. For a second, I thought I was going to sit down and be quiet, but then I changed my mind. I had to leave. No one seemed to have noticed the disturbance, except for some confused groups at tables near us. I didn't care.

"Enjoy your meal," I said to Frankie. I walked straight for the door. I was about to go into the hotel lobby when someone called out to me.

"Isobel." It was Antonia de Leon. She was seated at a table, with Paulo. I walked over stiffly.

"Good evening to both of you," I said. Paulo looked surprisingly uncomfortable.

"I have wonderful news," said Antonia. "You're one of the first to know."

I knew, somehow, exactly what the news was.

"Paulo and I are to be married next month." At first she seemed triumphant, but then she seemed frightened of me. Paulo shifted in his seat. I took Antonia's hand, tiny, white, and icy cold, and kissed her cheek.

"Congratulations," I said. I then took Paulo's hand and whispered in his ear. "If her feet are anything like her hands, she won't be much fun to share a bed with."

Paulo smiled, even laughed. He looked at me, admiringly. Antonia was upset, almost on the verge of tears. She wanted desperately to know what I'd said. Proud of myself, I pushed open the door and walked out into the lobby. I looked so strong, so controlled; I was like a dried bamboo pole, straight and smooth, hollow and dry as a bone, ready to break with the first strong wind.

"You knew it was coming. You knew it was coming," I whispered to myself as I walked through the lobby. I clenched my fists, promising myself that I wouldn't lose control until I was out of the hotel, and in a cab where no one could see me.

"I'm sorry, but this is my taxi," I said to the American couple waiting on the sidewalk. They didn't argue. I got in.

"Where to ma'am?" the driver asked me.

"Just around the block," I said. "I'm not really sure."

It wasn't fair. It wasn't right. Paulo was not Antonia's. She was a simpering fool with icy hands and the constitution of a canary. There had to be something I could do, some way I could change the situation. And then it dawned on me.

"Take me to Ermita," I said.

"Ermita?" asked the driver.

"Yes. I'll show you the way when we get there."

"Ma'am," said the driver, "you shouldn't go to Ermita alone."

"You're right. I shouldn't. Just take me there."

To drive through Ermita on a Friday, or on any

night, was no easy task. Taxis crawled down Mabini at a snail's pace, as men, Americans and Japanese, searched the street for the right girl for the evening. Some of the whores looked so young, it made me ill. I looked out the window, like the men in the cars in front and behind me, looking at every face of every girl and woman. The older women looked tired and mercenary, but the younger girls seemed hopeful, almost eager, waiting for someone to pull them out of this nightmare. We were moving so slowly that I could see through the open doors of the nightclubs and bars. I looked into the Kangaroo Club, the Australian bar. I saw a young woman seated on the lap of a man twice her size. He had blond hair and a meaty face. I tried to see what she looked like, but we were moving too fast.

"Turn right down here," I said.

"Ma'am, it's one way, ma'am."

"I'll get off here then." He seemed surprised, almost worried for me. I stepped out onto the street, black silk dress, heels. I knew people were watching me. While I was paying the driver, an American got into the cab with a particularly young girl. I looked at him, disgusted, until I caught his eye, but he was oblivious to me. He grinned out of the cab, smug, eager to be off to some motel. I turned off Mabini, walking away from the flashing lights and loud music, away from the tired women pacing up and down the street, mechanically, waiting for someone to pull over. The street I was walking on was poorly lit and seemed to be inhabited solely by very thin dogs. The dogs ran away when I came close to them, but only to the next trash can, until I drew near again. I had to walk carefully, since the street was riddled with potholes, potholes filled with stagnant water, and who knows what else. I could still hear the taxis and music from the main street, but it seemed further away than it really was. I felt as if I was in a dreamworld, alone, untouchable. I could hear a baby screaming in one of the apartments. There were very few lights in the windows, and the few I could see flickered, gas lamps. I tried to figure out which apartment the baby belonged to. I heard its wailing up and down the street. It could have been coming from anywhere. I turned the corner and found myself in more familiar territory, although I had never been there at night. I stopped at the third building. There were steps leading up to a cluster of small apartments. I watched a woman let herself out the front door. She was in a black sequined skirt, red satin heels, red sleeveless blouse, cut very low. She walked down the steps, glared at me, then headed toward Mabini. Another set of steps led down from the walk. I took these, five steps down, to a wooden door reinforced with iron bars. There was a small, faded wood sign tied to this with wire. It read:

MOTHER JOSEPHINE
PALMIST/DIVINER

I knocked on the door. It opened just a crack. I peered in, but could see no one. It was eerie, too eerie, but then I heard a voice about waist level.

"*Ano po?*" It was a young girl, about seven years old.

"Is Manang Josepina in?" I asked.

She nodded.

"Tell her Isobel della Fortuna is here to see her. Tell her it's urgent." The door was about to shut in my face, but I was able to wedge the toe of my shoe inside. I handed the child a five-peso bill. She snatched it and shut the door. I heard the bolt slide in place and then hurried footsteps as she ran along the corridor, frantic knocking, and then a door open and shut. She was in Manang Josepina's apartment. The next footsteps I heard were slow, a slight limp, the heavy thud of a cane. The door opened, and I saw the wise eyes of Manang Josepina peering up at me through the gloom.

"Isobel," she said. "An unexpected delight. Come in." She pushed open the door, letting some light filter in from the street.

"Ne Ne!" she called. The girl soon appeared with an oil lamp. We followed her down the hallway, our figures casting strange shadows along the walls, mine tall and slim, Manang Josepina bent, with her face peering onward, and Ne Ne, a child carrying a lamp almost as big as herself. At the end of the corridor was the shop, a place I had been to many times, but never at night, and never unannounced. The child fumbled with the knob, finally managing to open the door. The room was entirely dark, except for our lantern. Nothing had changed since my last visit. There was a crucifix, and a Buddha, and all kinds of things in bottles and boxes and jars on the shelves lining the walls. Odors of dampness and opium hung heavily on everything.

"Are there people in there tonight?" I asked, pointing to the room where she entertained the opium smokers.

"Not tonight. Tonight we are alone." She motioned for me to sit down. I sat on a chair in front of a small round table. The chair was covered with layer after layer of cloth, draped randomly. I was sitting on velvet. Manang Josepina took a similarly upholstered seat across from mine.

"What is so urgent?" she said. She took my hands in hers. She looked at my palms, one at a time, then together, and set them back on the table. This was not a good sign.

"You see it as well as I know it," I said. "Things have not been going well. It is as if I am cursed."

"Cursed? Who would curse you?"

"I can think of two people, offhand." I shrugged my shoulders. "It is possible."

"Ne Ne, fetch the urn and the pan," she said. Ne Ne came running over, carrying a brass urn and a silver pan with a highly polished surface. Manang Josepina set the pan on the table and poured some water from the urn inside. She then took a small bottle and shook a few drops of its contents into the bowl. She watched the liquid intently. I had long since given up trying to figure out just what she was doing, but she was always accurate, frighteningly so.

"You are not cursed by anyone, but this is a dark time for you."

I lit a cigarette and puffed nervously.

"You want an old lover back." She smiled at me, toothless, her eyes like two shiny black pearls.

"Yes, I would, but he's to be married," I said.

"You can win him back," she said. "I can help you."

"I thought that you probably could." All my previous visits had been for tarot-card readings and palmistry. The idea of leveling a curse or casting a spell had never crossed my mind.

"I have my ways. I won't bother you with them. They are both tedious and peculiar." She smiled again.

"No harm must come to him," I said. "But his fiancée . . ."

"I like to wonder who is more wicked, Isobel. You or I?"

"You are, by far, if only in your skill at executing

your intentions." I raised an eyebrow. "But tell me what you have in mind."

"I can't say he will marry you, but he will love you. His love of you will be a curse on him."

"And the fiancée, Antonia?"

"She is insignificant."

"All right," I said. "Go. Get him for me. I have nothing to lose. His name is Paulo Aguilar. Is that enough?"

"More than enough."

"Shall we agree on a price?" I asked.

"The value of this favor will be discussed when the work is done."

"You're very confident. I place my trust in you." I got up from the chair.

"Isobel, some words of advice before you leave. You say you have nothing to lose, but you have much to lose."

"Is that all?"

"No. Pay close attention to your dreams. Words of truth will come in the darkness."

I counted out five hundred-peso bills onto the table.

"For the advice," I said. Then I went out onto the street to catch a taxi. I had strange faith in her. I knew she would succeed, somehow, but her parting words disturbed me. I had much to lose. What did I have, save good health and sanity?

13

I am at the opera or the ballet. I'm not sure which. I don't know who I'm with either. Maybe I'm alone. The lights have dimmed, and no one speaks. I look down at the stage. There is a lonely stab of light in the darkness, a spotlight that falls on the stage illuminating a solitary woman. She is so familiar, so alone, and then I realize that it is I. I'm wearing a heavy brocade dress, Amy Puno's dress from *Mirandola*. It's so big, my shoulders come right up through the neckline, and it's difficult to keep the dress from falling down. I can hardly move. Around my neck are strings of pearls and precious stones. They're heavy and cut into my bare flesh. I see a male figure enter on the left. This is my cue to raise the fan to my face, but there are so many bracelets on my arm, gold, jewels, that this requires great effort. I look down at my wrist. It is thin, almost fleshless. I am emaciated. The faceless, nameless man is walking across the stage. I fan myself in slow painful moves, then I look down at my wrist. The skin is dry and wrinkled. It starts to split and peel back, leaving the bone exposed.

Then I'm in a large hall with no doors and no windows. There are white marble floors, and the walls are composed of *capiz* panels, which gives the room a strange glow. I'm in a white dress, ankle length. My feet are bare, and my hair hangs loose around my shoulders. I'm looking for a way out, and then I see the staircase, Gregorio's staircase. It rises out of the middle of the room, but where it ends, I can't see. I look at the ornate carvings on the banisters and runners. There are the same organic patterns, but they seem to be growing, coursing up and down the staircase, extending tendrils across the steps and back again. I step onto the stairs, trying to avoid the leaves and stems reaching out around me. After the third step, I turn to go back, but the branches have closed behind me. I can only go upward. I make my way to the top of the stairs, nervously. My dress catches on a thorny branch. It is torn in many places. There are brambles all around me. My hair has become tangled in a branch. I'm getting panicked. I start to free myself, but my hands fumble. Then I see it, crawling on the branch, an evil black snake. I pull away and struggle up the stairs, faster now. And finally I see the top. Standing there, alone, in a dark suit is Gregorio.

"Help me!" I'm screaming, loud, scared. He seems calm, too calm, then he raises his arm toward me. He's holding a gun. It's pointed at my head. I collapse onto the stairway.

I woke up with sweat pouring down my face. It was ten A.M., and the sun outside shone brightly, angrily. I lay in bed for about ten minutes, thinking over my dream, and then quickly got up. I put on the first clothes I found, a silver-gray pair of silk dress pants, a plain white T-shirt, and green lizard-skin loafers. I pulled the hair out of my face, tied it back with a nylon stocking that happened to be lying on the back of my chair, and raced out the door. I ran into my mother on the staircase.

"Isobel, where are you going?"

"Manang Josepina," I said.

"Like that?"

"Yes, like this." I tucked in the T-shirt.

"I'll go with you," she said.

"It's a private matter. I'd rather you didn't." I thought about this. "I insist that you don't." I walked down two more steps.

"You're keeping things from me," I heard her say, her voice trembling. "You don't love me anymore." I clenched my teeth. I knew that she was crying.

"Mother." I turned around. "It's not that I'm keeping things from you, I'm just in a hurry. That's all."

"All the people I love," she continued. "Your father went back to that monster." She raised the back of her hand to her mouth. "And now the only person I have left in the world."

"Mother . . ."

"Cold and distant." She started sobbing, leaning on the rail.

"Mother, I'm sorry," I said. "There really is nothing going on. It's just that I had a bad dream. It's nothing serious."

"Then why don't you want me to come?"

I bit my lower lip.

"Mother, you don't want to go into town. All the people pushing and shoving, the pollution. And the noise! Horns blaring, people shouting, all those little beggars pressing around you." I was starting to get through to her. "Besides, the traffic is just going to be incredible. The congestion, the crowding, the filth."

Mother looked at me nervously.

"I can't go," she said, almost apologetically.

"I'll make an appointment for Manang Josepina to come to the house."

"Good." She leaned on the banister, exhausted.

She looked so small and fragile. I felt guilty, because I'd scared her back into the house.

"Isobel, you will tell me everything that happens?"

"Of course, Mother, as soon as I get back."

The driver was gone. He was somewhere with Lourdes. I sent Auring down the street to fetch the taxi. Gregorio. What was he doing? Was he reading? Was he thinking about me?

Mabini was much different in the daylight. There were still the large and sweaty foreigners walking down the street in shorts and undershirts. They looked at me as I walked by, but I gritted my teeth and pretended to ignore them. The sun was beating down on me. I felt the top of my head. It was burning. I hadn't brought sunglasses. I hadn't really brought anything. I'd even forgotten my cigarettes. I squinted down the street, into the glaring sunlight. It was funny. The place had been easier to find in the evening. I walked slowly, adjusting my hair tie. I wondered if I should untuck my shirt, but decided that it wouldn't help my appearance.

Standing on the hot sidewalk, looking down the five steps that led to Manang Josepina's den, made it seem as if I was walking into a cool haven. I knocked on the door, anxiously, the image of Gregorio with the gun fixed in my mind. The door opened a crack. I looked down to see Ne Ne, sullen as always, peering up at me.

"*Si Manang Josepina,*" I said.

"Wala ho."

"Where did she go?"

"I don't know."

"Do you know when she'll be back?"

Ne Ne shook her head. I tried to collect my thoughts.

"Here," I said, taking a five-peso bill out of my wallet. I folded it in half and held it poised between my middle and index finger. "When she gets back, I want you to go down the street and telephone me. I must see her. It's very important. I'll come back when you call." I took a calling card out of my wallet and handed it to her, with the money. "There will be another five pesos when I return."

The child took the money. She blinked out at me from the darkness of the hallway, then abruptly slammed the door. I heard the bolt slide in place.

I walked back up the street, trying to imagine where Manang Josepina had gone. I pictured her in a bizarre outfit of feathers and shells, carrying a ceremonial rattle and a bottle of oil. She was tiptoeing outside Antonia's bedroom, peering over the windowsill, letting out an occasional rattle, while Antonia, covers drawn about her face, lay in bed frozen in terror. It was a pleasant thought.

Standing on the street corner, waiting for a cab, I realized how long it had been since I'd really talked to someone. Mother was waiting for me to come home, to tell her when Manang Josepina would visit the house, and whatever had transpired between us. She would be disappointed, I was sure, but I was glad that I wouldn't have to lie. Where was Manang Josepina, and what was I supposed to do? A taxi pulled over to the sidewalk, and I got in. I had to talk to someone desperately, then. I wanted to talk to Jorge. He listened. It wasn't guaranteed that he'd understand, but he would pretend that he did.

"San Lorenzo," I said to the driver. We were there in about twenty minutes. I got out, paid, then untucked my shirt, trying to stretch out the wrinkles. Standing at the gate, in the sunshine, it felt very strange. I couldn't recall ever having dropped by unannounced. I rang the bell. A maid answered the door.

"Is Señorito Jorge in?" I asked.

"*Wala ho.*" Again. Twice in one morning.

"Do you know when he'll be back?" The maid shrugged her shoulders. I heard the front door of the house open.

"Who is it?" I heard someone call out. It was Rosario.

"*Señorita della Fortuna, po,*" the maid answered.

"Show her in. Bring her into the house immediately."

I thought of refusing the invitation, but decided that it was not a good idea. I stretched at my T-shirt. It was still wrinkled. My pants were too shiny for daytime. My shoes didn't match anything, and my head itched. I walked inside the gate. Rosario had disappeared into the house. The maid motioned me to come inside. The first thing I saw was a large mirror. I looked haggard and nervous.

"I've seen you look better, Isobel." Rosario was leaning in the doorway. Her hair hung in front of her face, and there was a cigarette dangling in her left hand. I'd never seen her smoke, or look untidy. Her appearance shocked me. It was as if she had aged ten years since I'd last seen her. She brought the cigarette to her lips and coughed. Her large eyes seemed almost bovine now that she had lost weight. She looked up at me, sorowfully, as if I should hit her.

"I'm a mess," I finally agreed.

"It surprised me that you came here. I've always maintained that you're the only nonhypocrite in Manila," said Rosario. I had no idea what she was talking about.

"On the contrary, Rosario, I always fancied myself a devoted hypocrite." Rosario responded to this by either coughing or laughing. I couldn't tell which.

"Now that you're here," she said, "why don't we have a drink." She waved me into the next room with her right hand. "I know you drink, Isobel." This was true, but rarely at eleven A.M. I followed her into the living room and sat down beside her on the couch.

"Where is Jorge?" she said.

"I have no idea. I thought that he would be here."

"Where was he last night?"

"I haven't talked to him in a week," I said.

"What?" She lit another cigarette, which she held very stiffly between her fingers. "I can't believe that," she said. She really hadn't believed it. The maid came over with two drinks, amber-colored and smelling of sawdust. It was scotch.

"Rosario, what is going on? He hasn't called me in a week, which is why I came here, and you, drinking, smoking. I don't understand. Tell me. What is going on?"

She looked at me with the same bovine eyes. "Then it isn't you?"

"Me? Is he having an affair?"

Rosario lost her composure. She broke down into a fit of sobbing. She took the ashtray and hurled it across the room, knocking a picture frame off a table. The maid immediately replaced the ashtray, not seeming the least bit surprised, then disappeared into the kitchen, presumably to fetch the broom. Watching, I sat back on my end of the couch.

"He used to love me," she said, her eyes brimming over with tears. "But he doesn't anymore. He can't even look at me, he won't, and I haven't seen him in three days." She flung herself back on the couch, sobbing loudly.

"Have something to drink," I said, passing her the glass. She sat up and took a swig, then wiped her nose with a napkin.

"Liar," she said, with the vehemence of a child. "I know it's you. Everyone knows it's you. No one has seen you or Jorge anywhere in days. And when they do, you act so strangely. I know. I talked to Frankie Aguilar, and he told me what you were like."

"Frankie Aguilar." I shook my head. "Rosario, let's think this over logically. If I was having an affair with your husband, would I come to the house? Would I agree to sit down and have drinks with you?"

She looked at me suspiciously.

"No," I answered myself. "No, I wouldn't." She seemed unconvinced. I took a mouthful of scotch. "Rosario, I have no idea what's going on. The reason that everyone is seeing me act so strangely is because I've had a few bad readings from my fortune-teller. It makes me stressed, that's all. I'm just very high-strung lately."

She seemed to buy this. I almost believed it myself.

"Then where is Jorge?" she asked.

"I keep telling you, I don't know. I'm probably just as interested in finding out as you are"—I lit a cigarette—"and will possibly be more successful."

Rosario looked at me, confused. "I don't know what to think," she said.

"I can't promise you anything, but if I find out, or if Jorge calls me, I'll tell you." I called the maid over and told her to fetch me a taxi. "Rosario, you've been believing the worst. Maybe it's not that bad."

"Yes, it is. It is that bad. I can't do anything. I've

had to send the baby to stay with my parents, because I'm so nervous."

"Don't drink so much," I said, patting her arm. "You're forgetting that you don't drink." I got up and walked out into the hall, avoiding the mirror. My taxi arrived a short while later.

I got back to the house, and stood at the gate, waiting for the maid to let me in. I could focus on nothing but taking a shower. This was shaping up into one of the most arduous days in recent memory. Thinking of this made me bring to mind other trying days, and this constant rehashing of past miseries only made everything worse. I'd had a pounding headache all morning, which had strengthened since my visit with Rosario, possibly because of the scotch. I could manage a shower. That would make me feel much better, and then I was going straight to bed. I rang the bell. Auring answered. She seemed nervous.

"*Nandito si Señorito Jorge,*" she said.

"Jorge? What's he doing here?" I pushed past her and into the house. "Jorge!" I called, standing in the hallway. He came out of the living room. He was wearing dress pants and a crumpled white shirt. The top button was open, and his tie hung askew around his neck. He looked like he hadn't slept in days.

"Is that what you were wearing when you left your house three days ago?" I asked.

"Where did you hear that?"

"Guess," I said. He shrugged his shoulders. "I went

to your house, looking for you. Well, as you know, you weren't there. Rosario thinks it's me."

Jorge looked up briefly, shocked into attention, then passed quietly back into his melancholy.

"Jorge, what is going on?"

"Can we sit?" he asked me. He was thinking how to phrase what he had to tell me.

"It's that girl, isn't it?"

"What if it is?" he asked.

"Don't be so defensive. You wouldn't have come here if you didn't want to tell me."

"You're right, it's just that—"

"Jorge, just how old is she?"

He looked up at me, as if he'd just noticed that I was sitting there.

"You want to know," he said. "I'll tell you. She's sixteen. She's in high school. She is, was, absolutely innocent. I don't know what to do."

"You're in love with her, aren't you?" He was looking down at the tops of his shoes. "Jorge, tell me, are you in love with her?"

He was silent for a time. "If only I could marry her, but I'm married. I could get a divorce in Japan, but her parents still wouldn't let her marry me."

"Jesus, Mary, and Joseph, Jorge! You have to end this thing, now."

"I can't," he said. He shrugged his shoulders.

"You don't have a choice. What about Rosario?

She's turning into an alcoholic. And your baby, now with his grandparents."

"Don't give me that, Isobel. You're the one who told me to go along with this. You encouraged me, and now that it hasn't worked out, all of a sudden, you're the most righteous woman alive."

"Sure," I said, "I told you that it was all right. She's sixteen years old. I thought nothing of it. Everyone has affairs, but they don't destroy marriages, or people. Forget Rosario. Look at yourself. You look terrible."

"I've seen you look better," he said.

There was silence. Jorge stood up to leave.

"You know, Isobel, I don't understand you. People are people. They don't always behave the way they should, feel what they should. You can't just set them up to do things and then wash your hands when it backfires."

"This isn't my fault, Jorge," I said.

"Nothing ever is, is it?" He had his hand on the front doorknob, ready to leave.

"Jorge, don't go," I said. "I'm sorry. I have problems, too."

"I'm sure you do, Isobel," he said. "Best of luck."

And then he was gone. I knew I had lost him, because I could feel it in every part of my body.

14

I must have looked at the door for fifteen minutes before I realized that it was definitely closed. It was hard to tear myself away. Some sector of my brain told me that if I stood there long enough, Jorge would walk back into the house. Maybe he'd have a party to go to, or maybe he would want to have drinks with me or talk about things past. I knelt down on the marble floor, and lit a cigarette, still facing the door. The maid brought over an ashtray. An image flashed through my mind of Auring bringing me food, people having to walk around me to leave the house, the dogs sniffing me suspiciously as my fifteen-minute vigil rolled into hours, days, weeks. My silence was interrupted. Someone close by was crying. I looked behind me.

"Auring, why are you crying?" I said.

"It's so sad." She raised her hands to her face and ran into the kitchen.

I knelt there for a long time, although I'm not sure how long. Then, to my surprise, I heard a knock on the door.

"Come in," I said softly, expectantly.

The door opened just a crack at first, letting shafts of sunlight slice into the hall. The door swung open slowly, as if by its own accord, revealing the dark figure of Manang Josepina before a backdrop of early-afternoon sun.

"I must talk to you," she said. She offered me her hand, to help me up. It seemed strange to me that one so old and bent should help me. I felt weak, as if I was an invalid.

"When are things finally getting better?" I smiled wearily. "When will fortune smile on me?" She looked up at me intently with her dark eyes. I saw a light dancing there, in the two black pearls, and I knew she would be successful in our little endeavor.

"Fortune is a fickle patron," she said. "In one place she shines brightly while another is left in darkness."

"You always say that, and I always believe you." We walked to the living room. Manang Josepina stopped on the threshold. She put her cane just inside the door and looked to the right, and then to the left, as if she were looking for someone or something. She entered, and I followed her inside. As usual, she sat in the Spanish chair. It was mahogany, stained almost black, with a broad seat and high back. The carving was ornate, of flowers and vines, with a smiling satyr carved on the left of the back and a coy nymph on the right. There were huge clawed feet to the chair and a big red velvet cushion. Manang Josepina had difficulty getting into the chair, since it was so high. She inched herself back, holding her cane in her left hand as if it was a scepter, resting her right hand on one of the heavy scrolled arms. Her right hand was half-clenched, as always, because of arthritis. In the way she rested it, with her darkened curling nails and bulging knuckles, it seemed to echo the great clawed feet of the chair. It was as if it was her chair, where no one else should sit.

"I have been busy," she said to me, "very busy. I have been out all night, and soon we shall see the fruit of my efforts."

Out all night, yet she was still so alert, fueled by some source other than sleep.

"Can I get you something to drink?" I asked. "You must be hungry, too." She shook her head.

"There are more important things at hand. Get a pair of scissors," she said.

"Scissors?" She nodded, then waved me away

from her. I walked over to the highboy and took out a pair of silver scissors with finely patterned handles. They were never used, but rested in the drawer between the silver nutmeg grinder and silver candle snuffer.

"Will these do? I don't know how sharp they are."

She beckoned me over, nodding impatiently. I handed her the scissors, which she examined in the light.

"Good," she whispered. "Very good." I was nervous then, unsure of her for the first time. I realized how powerless I was against her.

"Come closer," she said. I took a step forward, aware of nothing but Manang Josepina and the scissors.

"Closer," she said. I could hear her breathing now, could see how deep the lines were in her face. "Don't be afraid. You must trust me." She reached out her hand and touched my hair, which hung down the left side of my face.

"I don't need very much," she said. "Just a little."

Her right hand still held the scissors. I saw them by my ear, out of the corner of my eye. Then I heard the shearing noise as they closed on my hair.

"Just a little," she said. I moved back, staring at the lock of soft black hair resting in the palm of her hand. My ignorance was overwhelming. She took a small bottle out of the pouch that hung around her waist and put the lock of hair inside. Then she took out two other bottles, both of which already contained strands of hair. One had shorter pieces, almost like dog hair, but the other one had hair like mine.

"Whose are they?" I asked.

"Paulo's." She held up one. "And Antonia's." She held up the other.

"What does it all mean?" I asked. She shook her head and put them away.

"I had a dream last night." I sat on the floor by her feet. "It was a bad dream. Do you know Gregorio del Pilar?" She nodded slowly, then smiled as if I'd just confirmed some private suspicion.

"I dreamed that he shot me. I was in a white dress, struggling up the stairs, the stairs in his house, only they were alive, grabbing me. And then I saw a snake, and then I saw him. He was standing at the top of the stairs with the gun pointed right at my head."

Manang Josepina didn't say anything. Her silence was making me nervous.

"My dress was all torn, and I was caught in a thorny bush, scratched and bleeding." I was babbling. She raised her hand to silence me.

"Gregorio del Pilar is in love with you."

"We don't know each other," I said, but I believed her. Somehow it made sense. "Oh my God, he's going to shoot me, isn't he?" I looked over my shoulder out the window. There was no one there. "He is, isn't he? He's going to shoot me." I covered my chest with my hands. "He can't shoot me. I can't die. I won't die." I got up and went over to the window. "He's out there somewhere now, with his gun, the gun he shot his brother with, and now he's looking for me."

Manang Josepina hammered her cane on the floor. I turned around, startled.

"Enough!" she said. "Be quiet. Sit down, and listen."

"I'm scared," I said. "Very scared. I won't leave the house."

"He will not kill you," she said sternly.

"But how do you know that? I saw him in my dream. I can see it now, clearly. I can feel it."

"It won't happen, because I won't let it happen."

"But how can you prevent it? You probably saw it before I even dreamed it." I was getting hysterical.

"You must trust me."

"But how can I when everything tells me to believe that he's out there, waiting for a chance to blow me away?"

"You will trust me, because you have no choice."

This was true.

"What are you going to do?" I looked at her, desperate.

"Do you have anything that belongs to him?" she asked.

"No." I shook my head.

"Think. Anything. Maybe you picked up a pen that

belonged to him, or perhaps he gave you a flower. Has he written to you?"

I racked my mind.

"Wait. He gave me his handkerchief." I turned and ran up the stairs to my room, not waiting for her response. I went to my dresser and pulled out the drawer where I kept my own handkerchiefs. I dumped its contents onto the bed, searching for a large plain handkerchief among the finely embroidered ones. There was one, but it belonged to Eduardo. I ran into the closet, opening all my handbags, pouring their contents onto the floor. Change, lipsticks, matches, earrings, all tumbled out in a heap on the floor, but no handkerchief.

"Think," I said out loud. "What did you do? What were you wearing?" And then it dawned on me. I had been wearing my houndstooth suit. I walked over to the rack where it hung and pushed back the other suits so that I could see it clearly. I reached into the left pocket of the jacket, which was empty, and then the right. It was there. I took it out. It was crumpled, but I could still feel the quality of the linen. I looked at it, aware of its importance. The embroidered letters *GDP* stared back at me. I walked down the stairs slowly, wondering what the consequences would be if I said I hadn't found it. I stopped at the door of the living room. Manang Josepina sat there, her eyes gleaming wickedly.

"Give it to me," she said. I hesitated before handing

it to her. She took it, held it briefly, then stuffed it unceremoniously into her pouch.

"You aren't going to hurt him, are you?"

"Why? Does he mean something to you?"

"No," I said, defensively. She got up from the chair and walked quickly to the door.

"Mother wanted to see you," I said.

"Another day. I have many things to do."

I followed her to the door. "I had another dream," I said. "I dreamed I was in a play. I was the lead, I guess, but I was emaciated."

She turned to me. "Isobel, everything comes with a sacrifice." And then she left. I leaned my face against the wall, my mind desperately trying to sort out the multitude of swirling thoughts. Then I heard my mother calling from upstairs.

"Isobel, who's there?"

"No one, Mother," I called back.

"Come, talk to me."

I went up the stairs to her room, stopping at the door. All the curtains were drawn.

"Come in," she said. She was lying in bed with her arm flung across her face. When I entered, she made an effort to sit up, propping herself on a stack of pillows.

"Mother, what is this? It isn't even three." She looked at me nervously.

"I wasn't feeling very well, so I took another pill. I get so sleepy."

"Mother, the doctor told you not to do that. Those pills are very powerful." She was looking up at me with heavy-lidded eyes. "Of course, I'm not telling you anything you don't know," I said to her. Or that will make a difference, I said to myself. I picked up the chair that was beside the door and stood it at the end of her bed. I took an ashtray and rested it on my knee.

"The room always smells of smoke after you've been here," Mother said.

"You smoke in here, too."

"But not like you," she said.

I shrugged my shoulders. "Where's Mando?" I asked.

"He's in the province."

"What's he doing there? Visiting his mother?"

"She's dead."

"I know that," I said. "I was being funny." She looked at me, nodding slowly.

"He's having an affair," she said.

"Doesn't that bother you? It used to bother you."

"No. I like it better when he's not around."

"Me too," I said. Mother looked up to the left, as she always did when trying to remember something.

"Tell me about Manang Josepina."

"She wasn't there. I left a message for her to call me. She was just at the house, but she had to leave."

"Tell me about your dream."

"My dream?" I said. "It was a bad dream."

"A bad dream? Tell me about it."

"It was a terrifying dream." I couldn't focus my mind at all.

"It's me, isn't it?" She pushed herself further up on the stack of pillows. "You won't tell me anything."

"Mother, it's not that. It's not that at all."

"You don't love me. You don't need me."

"Mother, on the contrary, I couldn't bear to lose you, especially not now. I need you." I was losing my composure, becoming agitated. She was the calm one, looking at me with pleading eyes.

"Why? Why do you need me now?"

"Because you're all I have left." I cut myself short.

"I'm all you have left? Isobel, what has happened?"

"Nothing," I said. "It's just that there is nothing like a mother. Mothers are special."

The very triteness of this last phrase confused her. She settled back into her pillows, watching me as if I might turn into something else.

"And Mother," I said, standing up from my chair, "I love you very much." I walked over to her and kissed her forehead, then turned and walked out of the room. I felt guilty for having confused her, but what else could I do? I couldn't tell her everything now. I walked back to my room, measuring my steps on the slate tile, one and a half tiles per step, one blank step, one line step. My room was exactly nine and a half steps from my mother's room, which was fourteen and one-fourth tiles.

Fourteen and one-fourth, I said to myself as I opened the door. The curtains were pulled, so I turned on the light. I noticed the phone on my desk. It was usually in Lourdes's room. I unplugged the phone from the cord. It was a good feeling. I then turned on all the lamps in the room. There were five. One on my desk, one in the corner near the houseplant, a tall brass one beside the rocking chair, and one set up to illuminate a portrait of my mother, a rather sketchy likeness, but one that she liked. I wondered if I'd ever had all the lamps on at once. It was so bright that I could almost hear the brightness ringing in my ears. Then I started to unplug them, one by one, walking around the room, pulling the cords. The room grew quiet, still, then finally I achieved the silence of total darkness.

15

I was in the car speeding down to Batangas. I held Paulo's letter in my hand. Slowly I unfolded it, for the tenth time in as many hours. The creases had made the paper weak, and the page was tearing along one of the folds. The handwriting was regular, and upright, small with occasional jots upward. It read:

> Dear Isobel,
> I have been meaning to write to you for a long time, but as you know, I have been very busy. Please don't think me too gruesome. It isn't that I've forgotten

about you. Other things seem to have come up, things which have needed my attention, but I would like to see you. Since it would not be to either of our advantage to be seen together in Manila, I would like to meet you in our house in Calatagan, Batangas. I know this is abrupt. I would rather it not sound that way, but as I'm sure you know, it is very difficult for me to write this letter.

What I propose is that you meet me in Calatagan on Wednesday. I will send my driver to your house at ten A.M. He will drive you to Batangas if you choose to come. If you decide to ignore my invitation, I understand. I know I haven't said much, but I would really like to see you.

Love,
Paulo

I folded the letter and put it back in the envelope.

I was excited when I first got the letter. I felt that things had finally come together, that everything was beginning to pay off. Finally, something good was happening. I rushed into my mother's room to tell her. I read the letter to her as she lay in bed. As I walked around her she watched me and babbled about what clothes I was going to bring and how long I was going to stay.

"Isobel," she finally said, interrupting me, "he's still getting married, isn't he?"

"Yes," I said.

"You don't want that. I don't want that for you." I knew that she understood the situation well, but I lied to her and myself, saying that this had to be different. It was different, but Mother just shook her head.

"I know you're disappointed. I'm sorry," I finally said, "but no one's going to marry me anyway. I might as well be friends with an Aguilar." Mother didn't try to talk me out of going. I think that she finally realized that she'd lost, that we'd lost, to something bigger than the both of us. People were not willing to forget who I was. I could be the most beautiful woman in Manila, but I'd still be Isobel della Fortuna, lucky to have any name at all.

"I wanted so much more for you," she said. "It's all my fault." But I had no time to listen to this. It was ten, and time for me to leave.

"It's not your fault," I said. "It's nobody's fault. It isn't even a problem." And then I left.

I could see the driver's eyes in the rearview mirror, and I knew that he was looking at me.

"How much longer?" I asked.

"We're close, ma'am, very close."

I looked out the window. There were coconut palms everywhere. Stands selling *buko*, young coconut, lined the road.

"Are there many communists here?" I asked the driver.

"Yes." He nodded vigorously. "NPAs, the New

People's Army, you know. It's very dangerous to travel at night."

"At night," I said. "And in one of the Aguilar's cars."

He smiled when I said this, a big smile. One of his front teeth was missing and the other was framed in gold. It made him look odd.

"The Aguilars own all this land"—he gestured to the left—"but they are not popular."

"Are you from here?" I asked.

"I am from a village ten miles south of Calatagan. I am the wealthiest man in that town, and I am not rich." I looked at the driver closely. His face was dark brown with deep furrows and wrinkles over his brow and the sides of his face. It was as if he had been carved out of wood.

"Do you know Señorito Paulo well?" I asked. The driver nodded.

"I always drive him. He tells me everything." I seriously doubted this. We turned and entered through a heavy stone-pillared gate. The gravel road was bumpy now. On either side of us tall walls had been erected, and the road was lined with fragrant frangipani trees.

"Does this all belong to the Aguilars?" I asked.

"No. That belongs to the Casinos, and that"—he pointed to the right—"is the de Leons'." I saw a glimmer in his eye as he said this. He watched for some sign of jealousy, but I gave him none. I sat quiet and composed, and lit a cigarette.

"Are we nearly there?" I asked.

"This is their property, and there, at the top of the hill, is their house." It was a surprisingly modern house, a rectangular box sitting at the peak of a hill lush with vegetation. The car pulled up right to the front door. I got out, looking briefly to my right and my left, then walked up the steps. A very fat old maid showed me into the vestibule.

"Are you tired?" she asked. I shook my head. "Please sit down." I sat on a wooden bench. A younger maid came over with a mirror and wash-basin on a tray. A towel was draped across her arm.

"Freshen up," said the older maid. I washed my hands and face and patted myself dry with the towel. Things were so different in the province than they were in the city.

"Where is Señorito Jorge?" I asked.

"He's at the stable. He just bought a new horse, white, a ladies' horse, with long slim legs." She looked at me and smiled. "You're as pretty as he said you were, but so thin, and a little pale, but in time . . ." She wiped her hands on her skirt, looking at me as if I were a piece of land she was surveying.

"You're very kind," I said, "but is there anywhere I can be alone? Much as I appreciate all this attention, it's making me dizzy." I looked over to a doorway on my left where six maids stood, falling over one another, each trying to get a better look at the señorito's new mistress.

"Of course," she said. "I'll take you to the library. Señorito knows that you've arrived, and should be here any second now." She showed me to the room, pausing before she left. Her look seemed to say: "A little too pale, and a little too thin, but other than that, quite satisfactory."

There were very few books there for a room that was supposed to be a library, very few books, and very few shelves. There was, however, a card table, chess, and a backgammon set, and at least three different kinds of cigars on display. I felt that I had entered the alien world of men. It was very strange. I went over to the chess set and picked up a black pawn, turning it over carefully in the palm of my hand.

"Isobel."

I turned around. Paulo was standing in the door in full riding regalia. He wore breeches and boots and was holding his hat by the strap, his crop tucked neatly under his right arm.

"Paulo, you look absolutely ridiculous, like one of those Filipino Anglophiles. You'll never be white." I smiled.

"Ah. How sad my life is. Money, power, beautiful women. Only royalty and whiteness seem to elude me." I put the chess piece down. "You look very well for someone whom I've heard is an alcoholic, a drug addict, and on the verge of a nervous breakdown," he said.

"Is that what you've heard?"

"Common knowledge." He offered me his arm. "Come into the garden. I have something to show you."

We walked together back through the vestibule, past the giggling maids, down the steps. Standing a short distance from the house, held by a nervous groom, was a magnificent white horse.

"What do you think?" asked Paulo.

"Impressive." I let go of his arm and walked over to the horse. I patted the pinkish nose, soft as velvet. The horse jerked his head back a few times, but then settled down, watching me with large soulful eyes.

"Quite beautiful," I said, looking at Paulo over my shoulder.

"A fine horse." He walked over and ran his hand down the right front leg of the horse. "A good jumper."

"Where did you get him from? There aren't that many Arabians around here."

"No, there aren't," he agreed. "I called in a favor, something which the Iranian ambassador owed my father." Paulo winked at me. "He was more than willing to get it for me. It's a ladies' horse." He smiled at me.

"I could see you on it," I said. I patted the shoulder. "Not that you're much of a rider."

"I didn't get it for myself."

"Antonia?"

"She can't even ride a bicycle. Can you see her five feet off the ground, going twenty miles an hour on a horse? Isobel, this is for you."

Stunned, I took two steps back and then walked into the house. Paulo knew better than to follow me. He stayed behind, leaving me time to adjust to my new role as Isobel, favored mistress.

The next three days were filled with the same bewildering attention. I can't say exactly what was going on in my mind. I tried to avoid thinking, because that always led to thoughts of the future, and that was such an unstructured void. Nothing much happened, nothing that is interesting to tell. I rode my horse, and ate well. Everyone babied me, catered to every desire I had, even Paulo, but I found it hard to relax. There was something about the very idyllic nature of this time that put me on edge.

"Don't be so suspicious," said Paulo. "It's not as if you don't deserve it."

By Saturday I was extremely tense. At lunch, I knocked over a glass of wine, leaving a deep red stain on the white linen cloth, and then for some inexplicable reason, burst into tears.

"Isobel, stop, please. It's not the first time you've spilled something," said Paulo. "I don't understand. What do you want?"

But I couldn't say, because I didn't know. Paulo

was frustrated and left the table. By dinner time, I had apologized, and he accepted this, although he knew that my nerves were still frayed. After dinner we played backgammon. He seemed to think that Cointreau was the answer to my distress, and kept my glass filled, but I knew that what I felt was real. Something was going to happen. It was a running consciousness that I could not escape. At around eight, Puring, the older maid, entered the library. She seemed confused.

"There is a phone call," she said. "It's for Señorita Isobel."

"Isobel," asked Paulo, "did you tell anyone that you were coming here?"

"No," I said. "My mother, but she doesn't know exactly where I am, and she wouldn't call anyway, unless something were wrong."

I got up from the table and went out into the hallway to the phone. Paulo stood, leaning in the doorway, watching me.

"Hello?" I said.

"Isobel, it's Lourdes."

"Lourdes, how did you know I was here?"

"Auring saw you leave with Paulo's driver. I had her go to his house and find out the address, from the help, of course. No one knows."

"What is it?"

"It's Mother. She overdosed. She's in the hospital, Makati Medical Center."

"Did she ask for me?"

"No, she didn't ask for you." Lourdes sounded bored.

"How bad is it?"

"I don't think I should say over the phone."

"Lourdes, damn it, how bad is it?"

"Don't raise your voice at me, Isobel, I'm doing you a favor."

"Jesus Christ. How bad is she?"

The phone went dead. She had hung up. I looked at the receiver, then set it back on the phone.

"Paulo," I said, surprisingly calm, "I have to go to Manila, now."

"Why?"

"My mother OD'ed. I have to go."

"You can't," he said. "Too many NPAs."

"But I have to go."

"I can't let you go," he said. He glanced at his watch. "Wait until morning, seven hours."

"Seven hours may be too long." He turned his back to me and started walking into the library.

"Either I go now with your blessing, and come back, or I go now without it, and give you back to Antonia."

"What kind of choice is that?" He shrugged his shoulders. "Have it your way."

Five minutes later, I was ready to leave. Paulo was standing at the door. I could hear the car engine running outside.

"Wait," he said, stopping me as I ran out the door. "Take this." He handed me a gun, a revolver. "Have you tried one of these before?" I nodded. I'd fired an air pistol once. "I hope to God you don't have to use it," he said. I ran down the steps and got into the car. It was the regular driver. He seemed very nervous, the furrows in his face were even deeper than I remembered them.

"I want you to drive very fast, as fast as you can," I said.

"Yes, ma'am," he answered, and pulled out of the driveway, down the gravel road. We passed the armed guard at the gate. He saluted to us, and we left the safety of the Aguilars' stone walls. I felt the gun cold in my hand, as cold as my mother's hands. Soon we were on the highway. It would take us at least two hours to get back to Manila. I wasn't sure what would greet me there, but I sensed that I had not overestimated the urgency of the situation. The image of my mother's tired face was fixed in my mind. I checked the speedometer. We were going eighty-five miles per hour, but then we were going seventy, and then fifty, and then thirty-five.

"What is going on?" I shouted. "Why are we slowing down?"

"Lights ahead," said the driver. "We're going to have to turn back."

"Turn back? What are you talking about? Maybe it's just a military checkpoint."

"Not there. That isn't army. Remember, I'm from here."

"Communists?"

"Yes, NPAs, or maybe armed robbers," he said.

I panicked then. He was really going to turn back.

"Keep going," I instructed him. I raised the gun so that he could see it.

"It's too dangerous." He shook his head.

I was getting angry. "You're going to drive on," I said. "Either they're going to shoot you, or I'm going to shoot you. They don't expect us. We'll be going ninety miles per hour. I'm six inches from your head, going nowhere, and can always drive myself." I wasn't joking. I could see a film of perspiration on the back of his neck. He stole a nervous look in the mirror.

"I'm serious." The car started forward suddenly. It's hard to describe exactly what happened after that. There was a blaze of light. I lay down on the seat, instinctively. I heard some rapid-fire shots, and the sound of shattering glass. It was the rear window. Luckily, the glass didn't splinter. The bullet entered cleanly, then went through the window of the passenger seat in front. The explosion of light and sound stunned me. I felt us slide off the road, into a depression, but the driver regained control. I sat up again and pushed the hair out of my face. We were back on the road, speeding faster than ever, north to Manila. There was silence for almost the entire trip. The driver looked pale, I thought, and I felt sorry for him.

"I'm sorry for endangering your life," I said.

He looked at me as if I was absolutely insane.

"My mother is very sick," I said. This seemed to confirm his worst suspicion. "Good thing the back window didn't fall on top of me. I know you can't see out of it, but we're still lucky." I realized how stupid I sounded. Neither of us wanted to talk. I leaned back in the seat and thought about my mother. What was wrong with her? But far worse than that, why hadn't I been there? Why had I neglected her? I had left her in Manila with no one, in a dark room, lying alone in her huge bed, or maybe propped up on pillows, thinking about times past and what had gone wrong.

"We're here, ma'am," the driver said. Makati Medical Center loomed above me, glowing from every window, like a beacon. I got out of the car and looked around. People were staring at us. I remembered the state of the car, bullet-holed and muddy, and then I noticed that I was still carrying the gun. I threw it back onto the backseat of the car and shut the door.

"What are you all staring at?" I said. This only seemed to get more people's attention. I escaped into the building. Auring was standing at the reception desk, tearfully arguing with a nurse. She called out when she saw me.

"They won't let me see her," she said.

"Family only," said the nurse. She was most unsympathetic.

"I'm her daughter." The nurse eyed me briefly. "Sixth floor. Room 624, to your left as you exit the elevator."

I got into the elevator with twelve other people and found myself standing next to a very fragrant, powdered, coiffed woman, thirtyish I thought. The elevator ride seemed extraordinarily long, especially since the woman eyed me the entire time. It made me uncomfortable. We both got off at the sixth floor and walked together, though a respectful three feet apart, down the corridor to Mother's room. There was a crowd of people around the door, mainly Mando's friends and relatives, but Mother's sister Tita Allesandra was there. She was kneeling a few feet from the door, deep in prayer, oblivious of all that was around her. Lourdes came over when she saw me.

"How did you get here so quickly?" she asked.

"I left immediately after you called."

"But isn't it dangerous?"

"Yes. Yes, it is. Can't I go in and see Mother?"

"No one's stopping you."

She was right. I was stalling on my own.

"But maybe I should warn you," Lourdes started.

"Warn me?"

Lourdes looked up at me nervously, but she couldn't finish her sentence. She showed me the door.

There was no one in the room with Mother. She was lying, asleep, in bed, and seemed perfectly peaceful, almost too peaceful. I pulled a chair up beside the bed.

"Mother, Mother, it's Isobel." There was no response. I took her hand. It was cool, even cooler than usual. My eyes clouded over with tears.

"Mother." I tried again, no response. I could hear her breathing. I took her hand and put it next to my feverish face, sitting hunched over like this, trying to understand what was going on. I felt drained.

"Mother, I've been meaning to talk to you, but I couldn't because nothing good was happening. But now things are getting better, much better."

"You know she can't hear you." I turned to see Lourdes standing in the doorway.

"Maybe when she wakes up."

"Isobel, I don't think you understand."

"What?" I said, but at that moment I understood. I got up from my chair and walked over to Lourdes. "Tell me. Get up the courage and tell me. Why are you so hesitant? It's not your fault, so why don't you tell me?"

"The doctor's outside."

"The doctor can go to hell."

"I don't have to listen to this." She walked out of the room.

"Yes, you do," I said, following her. Out in the corridor, I saw Mando standing with the powdered, coiffed lady from the elevator.

"Lourdes, who is that?"

She looked at me and then lowered her eyes.

"No. You're going to tell me this." I grabbed her arm. "Yes, you are." I could see my knuckles turning blue as I squeezed her arm tightly. "Now, Lourdes, who the hell is that?"

"That's Papa's mistress."

"What is she doing here? What the hell is she doing in Manila?" Lourdes looked up at me briefly, then down at her feet.

"She's staying with us."

"In the house?"

She nodded.

"With Mando?"

She nodded.

"*Bastardo,*" I whispered to myself. I started to walk slowly toward Mando and the woman.

"*Bastardo,*" I called to him. "Is this the whore that you invited to live in our house?"

"Isobel, calm down," said Mando. He raised his hands defensively. And then I flew at him, at them. I don't exactly know what I intended to do. I think I was trying to strangle them both, and thought myself quite capable of doing this. I did manage to bruise the side of his face before his relatives pulled me back.

"You bastard," I screamed, struggling to get free, "I'll kill you. With my bare hands, I'll kill you."

"Look," he shouted, pointing at me. "She's crazy. Just like her mother, absolutely crazy." He made a safe distance between the two of us. I had clearly terrified him. I turned to Lourdes.

"Defend him," I said. "Just try. Remember, she's your mother, too, and she's lying there, unconscious, because of him."

She looked at me, frightened, guilty. Then I broke down and started crying, kneeling on the floor of the hospital, wailing, like the women at funerals, as if my whole body would break open. I cried in anger, not self-pity, screaming as if I was a wild animal. The people cleared a circle around me, watching nervously, and then, when I was quiet, some nurses came and took me downstairs. Auring was still there, pleading with the nurse. I took her arm.

"Auring, it's time to go home." We walked out of the hospital together and waited for the car.

16

Lourdes stood watching me at the door of my room.

"Why are you packing?" she said. "You have no place to go."

I put down the shirt I was folding and looked at her. "I really don't need this right now."

"Papa's in the province. He won't be back for another two weeks at least."

"Why?"

"Because he thinks you're going to kill him." I

smiled for the first time in four days. "You can stay," she said.

"Lourdes, sit down," I said. "You don't have to be nice to me. In fact, I don't want you to be nice to me."

"Why?"

"Because you were never nice to me before, and if you start now, I'm going to begin to think that you feel sorry for me."

"What's wrong with that?"

"I hate it, so stop. That's all."

She got up and left the room. I felt another wave of self-pity coming on, so I started packing faster, throwing everything into the suitcase; shirts, shoes, bags. Then I couldn't get it closed. I tugged at the cover of the suitcase, but I knew it wouldn't all fit. I tugged at it anyway.

"Isobel, it's not all going to fit," Lourdes said, back at the door.

"Did you come just to tell me that?"

"No," she said. "Paulo's downstairs. He's waiting for you in the living room."

When I entered the room, he was sitting on the couch with a glass of scotch. He looked upset, or as upset as I had seen him sober. His eyebrows were set further down than usual, and he was pouting.

"I noted the unusually large contribution of flowers in my mother's room from the Aguilar family. All white lilies, as if she was dead. Everyone thinks you're a family of perverts now. The only other person who sent white lilies was my father, excuse me, my Tito Vince. No one else seems to care that they're her favorite kind."

"But they are. You told me that several times."

"I also told you that I didn't like flowers, but I was lying."

"Well," he said, "you look extraordinarily calm for someone who went stark raving mad last Sunday night. Did you really threaten to kill him?"

"With my bare hands." I sat beside him on the couch. "What's been happening with you?"

He took a deep breath and looked at me as if he had something difficult to say.

"Go ahead," I said. "It's not as if you'll ruin my week."

"No. On the contrary, I think this is more my problem than yours."

"Good."

"It's Antonia. She found out about our little rendezvous, through one of the maids."

"That isn't very surprising."

"No, it isn't, but she had a tantrum," he said. He had his face resting on his hands now. "She tried to call off the wedding."

"But of course she didn't mean it."

"Of course not," he said. "But she screamed just loud enough for the parents to get involved. They moved up the wedding date."

"For when?"

He gave me another nervous look. "Next Sunday."

"But that's only ten days from now."

"I know," he said.

"You've only been engaged for two weeks."

"Three weeks tomorrow, but as far as my parents are concerned, we've been engaged since I was two."

"That's awful." I felt genuinely sorry for him. "How about your honeymoon?"

"That's one good thing that came out of all of this. We were supposed to go to Europe, but now since there's no time to plan it, we're going to Hong Kong."

"Hong Kong?" I started laughing.

"It's not where you are," said Paulo, "it's who you're with." He took a gulp out of the glass and set it on the table, then he checked his watch. "I have to go."

"Where?"

"To the tailor's. I need a new suit."

"I guess I won't be seeing much of you over the next week," I said.

"No, but you're invited to the wedding. I even found you a date. Guess who your date is."

"Your cousin."

"Frankie? I hadn't even thought of that."

"Then don't. Who is it?"

"Monching. He can't wait." I saw Paulo to the door, then went upstairs to get ready for the hospital. I felt myself walking with the same tired steps as my mother. I paused at the top of the stairs, not breathless, but feeling that I should be. I looked down, imagining Mother in a white dress with a blue sash, her hair smoothed back, walking from the kitchen out the front door on her way to Mass. Then I heard noises coming from her room. I got up and walked over slowly, almost expecting it to be Mother pottering around, but it was just Lourdes. She was throwing Mother's cosmetics into a box, clearing the dresser.

"Stop that," I said.

"But Papa said . . ."

"I don't give a damn what that father of yours said. They're not moving in here."

"But he said . . ."

I took her by the shoulders. "Your mother hasn't even been in the hospital for a week, and you're burying her. She isn't dead. Do you hear me?" Lourdes said nothing. I shook her.

"Yes," she said, stuttering in terror.

"You idiot," I said, letting her go. "What do you think I'm going to do? Kill you?"

She turned around and ran into her room next door. I started putting the bottles back on the dresser, dusting some of them off with my sleeve. Then I heard Lourdes crying in her room. I walked quietly into the hallway and listened at her door. She was on the phone with Mando.

"She's going to kill me," she said. She was sniveling.

"Now is that absolutely necessary?" I asked. I walked over and took the phone. "Hello, Mando," I said, but he hung up immediately. "Yes, I think it's probably a good idea if you leave for a while. Maybe you can stay with Tita Mercedes. I'll help you pack."

I walked over to Lourdes's chest of drawers and opened the top drawer. Pastel cotton underwear was neatly folded, artfully arranged. "How many do you think you'll need?" Lourdes had filled her arms with an assortment of clothes from her closet and seemed to have trouble answering me. "Maybe it would be better if I called Auring to help you?" She nodded emphatically. "Auring!" I called down the stairs. I stood at the balcony and watched her exit the kitchen, wiping her hands on the front of her dress. She started quickly up the stairs, but seemed to lose momentum with each additional step. At the top of the stairs, she burst into tears.

"I'm sorry, ma'am, but I just can't, not yet," she said.

"Maybe you'll be able to come upstairs tomorrow."

She nodded.

"Are you coming with me to the hospital?"

She nodded.

"You can go now." I said. She turned around and went back down the stairs.

"Why is everyone so goddamn weak?" I shouted. "Sniveling, pottering around, carrying on like it's the end of the world. Well, it isn't. It isn't over yet."

I heard Lourdes bolt her door shut. I went over and knocked softly. "Lourdes?" There was no answer. "Lourdes, I know you're in there." Nothing. "I just wanted to tell you that I'm leaving for the hospital in fifteen minutes and should be gone at least an hour and a half. It might be a good time for you to leave."

Nothing had changed at the hospital. Mother lay still on the bed, her hair neatly combed, arms by her sides, surrounded by dozens of lilies. Auring burst into tears the moment she entered the room. This was good, because it gave me a reason to send her out. I told her to go kneel in the hallway with Tita Allesandra, who seemed to have become part of the hospital furnishings, like a chair or a houseplant. I sat by Mother's bed, unsure of why I was there. I took her hand, which was cool, but the chances of her waking up now were so slim that it had lost its appeal. I set it above her head on the pillow, then messed up her hair. It was much better this way. I spent the next hour in thought, but somehow managed to think only of things trivial, such as what I was going to wear to Antonia's wedding, and where I should say Lourdes was if anyone should call. Then it was time to go. I set Mother's left arm askew and messed up her hair some more. Outside the door, Tita Allesandra and Auring were still deep in prayer.

"Auring," I said, "it's time to go."

It's strange how rapidly people can reschedule their lives, rearrange everything into its proper place, turn a tragedy into something as mundane as brushing one's teeth. Now reality had begun to set in. I no longer thought of this time as visiting Mother. I now thought of it as rearranging Mother, adjusting an arm, and messing her hair, giving life to something that was, for all intents and purposes, dead. I couldn't sleep that night, even with the knowledge that none of my evil family were in the house. I got out of bed, in my nightgown, and went down to the dining room. My cigarettes were on the table somewhere. I felt for them, and then for the lighter. It was very relaxing, smoking in the dark. The darkness was reassuring. It almost seemed to absorb things. Everything lost its identity in the dark.

"Ma'am?" I heard Auring ask, into the dining room.

"No, Auring," I said, "it's just Isobel."

This was my dream. I'm sitting with my mother in the hospital, holding one of her delicate hands, so cool, watching the sheets on her chest rise softly with each labored breath. Her eyes are closed. I can hear Tita Allesandra's prayer filtering through the door, but somehow echoing throughout the room.

"Please save my sister, dear God, in her innocence and tragedy, in her fragile reality and undeniable beauty."

But there is no hope in her prayer. It is as if the prayer is more a condemnation of Mother's endless sleep than a plea for escape. Then it changes.

"Please save Isobel in her innocence and tragedy, in her fragile reality and undeniable beauty."

It makes me angry. I leave my mother, letting her hand fall limply off the bed. I walk purposefully to the door, flinging it open, hearing the prayer reverberate throughout the hall.

"Please save Isobel . . ."

But I am no longer in the hospital. I am in a garden, or jungle, alone, cold, but I can still hear the prayer.

". . . in her innocence and tragedy, in her fragile reality."

I stop suddenly, aware of something watching me. I see a gibbon, majestic, white, peering at me through the leaves. He leaps from his perch, swinging strongly through the leaves, mouth open in a piercing scream. He comes fast, breaking branches, tearing vines. I stand frozen in my place, unsure of what to do, my mouth open to scream, but no sound coming out. The gibbon is close now. I see he is unchained, and crazed. He comes so close that I can feel his breath on my face, hear his heart beating in some remote corner of my brain, sense his strength and tension.

My hands fly up to my face protectively, and finally I call out. But I am alone, in my room. There is only me, sitting up in bed, my heart racing. It is dark outside, but I can sense the coldness and strength of the coming day.

17

The wedding was held in a small church in Greenhills. I'm sure that Antonia would have prefered Manila Cathedral, or any one of those wedding churches, but under the circumstances, she was lucky to get this. The church was nice, but small, and on this Sunday morning, very very crowded. Monching and I were seated toward the back of the church with the guests of the groom. I had the aisle seat, which I needed that day because it was so warm. I recognized the woman next to Monching. I had sat next to her once at Mass. Once more, she had remembered her fan, and I had forgotten mine. She fanned herself dramatically, sharing the breeze with the man beside her. Monching was wiping the perspiration off his face with a handkerchief. His baggy silk suit was neither black, nor silver, nor purple, but somehow a combination of the three. I wore a simple white dress. I looked around at the people sitting in this hot little church. They were trying to be discreet, but nevertheless, were looking at me, seated with the guests of the groom in a white dress.

"Monching, I want to leave," I said. "I can't seem to remember why I came here."

"You came here because you were invited. You came here because I was coming," he answered. But neither of these reasons satisfied me. Maybe I was here to embarrass Antonia. That seemed the most likely. That was why Paulo had invited me, I thought, but I just didn't care about her anymore. She was, as Manang Josepina had said, insignificant. Then the organ music began. The entire congregation turned to see the bride entering from the rear of the church. Antonia stepped into view, hanging on to her father, who was only a few inches taller than she was, and a good deal shorter than everyone else. Antonia's dress was just as I had imagined it, a mass of lace and frills.

"Are we sure she's in there?" I asked Monching. He laughed.

Antonia struggled down the aisle in her dress, supported by her father. Mr. de Leon held his head high and stuck out his chest as if he were trying to puff himself out to twice his normal size. Then they were walking right beside me. Antonia saw me, and was surprised. She looked away, down at her flowers, or something, but it was strange. Her entire face was covered with a rash. There were red splotches all over her skin.

"Monching, what on earth is the matter with Antonia?" I asked.

"I don't know," he whispered back. "No one does. They think she's been *kulamed.*"

"*Kulamed?* Who on earth would go through the trouble of putting a hex on her?"

"I don't know," said Monching. "I thought that you might." He was fishing, but I said nothing. There was a time when I would have been glad to accept the credit, but now I felt nothing for her, except pity. I spent the rest of the ceremony focusing on various things around the church, the arrangements of pink roses and baby's breath, the ornately carved beams on the ceiling, and the clasp of the necklace on the woman in front of me. I paid no attention to what was going on, to what part of the ceremony was happening. I didn't want to know. I just wanted it to be over. Finally, the wedding was over. I must have been the third person out of the building. I found myself standing next to Monching, surrounded by a mob of very short people, which I took to be the de Leon contingent. Paulo and Antonia came out of the church. Paulo smiled at everyone, and Antonia was waving excitedly in her usual quick agitated moves, which always reminded me of a bird. She took her bouquet and prepared to throw it. I got ready, but she saw me, and threw it to the other side.

"She's a poor sport," I said. Monching chuckled, rocking back and forth, his thumbs stuck deeply into his purple cummerbund. And then it was time for the reception.

The reception was held at the Aguilar house, in the garden. There were the same pink roses everywhere, and the same herds of dwarflike de Leons. A singer stood a short distance away. She was accompanied by a piano, which had been rolled out of the living room and into the yard. I heard her singing "J'ai deux amours," which seemed oddly appropriate. It struck me as odd that she should have chosen such a song. Since I was standing with Monching, we stood by the hors d'oeuvres. His favorite was the warmed Brie on apple slices. He'd already finished an entire plate, but sent the maid back for more.

"Not a bad turnout," he said.

"No," I agreed. "I saw Eduardo with someone. They looked bored."

"They were bored," said Monching. "Bored, and boring."

"You know who I've been looking for is Jorge. I'd love to see him," I said.

"Oh my, Isobel, you are out of touch. It's absolutely understandable, with your mother in the hospital and everything."

"Monching," I interrupted, "where is Jorge?"

"He's in Hong Kong."

"What is he doing in Hong Kong?"

"It's a sad business," said Monching, stuffing more Brie in his mouth. "He eloped with that sixteen-year-old. Even worse, he met her at one of my parties."

"Oh, my God," I said. "And what of Rosario?"

"Well, I've heard all sorts of stories." He grimaced. "Nothing too reliable. Some say she's become an alcoholic, but I find that hard to believe."

I closed my eyes, as if that would make everything go away.

"Isobel, are you all right?"

"Fine, just a little surprised."

"I thought you'd know. I hate to be the one to tell people things like that." He was lying. "But I've been meaning to ask you, Isobel. How are things between you and Paulo?"

"I've never gone out with a married man," I said.

"Well, there's a first time for everything, but you must be happy. It is what you wanted."

"I didn't realize what it was going to cost me."

"What do you mean?"

"Nothing. I don't know." I shrugged my shoulders.

"Being with Paulo is almost like being with myself. We're cynical, we're superior, we're arrogant. It's impossible for anyone to deal with us, so we deal with each other. He must be one of the only people, if not the only person in Manila who respects me, but I wonder if he respects anyone else. It's not as if we're in love. Rather, we're condemned to one another since we can't get along with anyone else."

"It sounds so interesting, so involved," said Monching. He hadn't really been listening.

"Monching, I don't know how long it's going to last. Sometimes I think I hate him."

"Nonsense," said Monching. "I can't wait until all this wedding hubbub dies down so that Paulo can start bringing you to all the parties."

"Monching," I said, laying my hand on his plump shoulder, "the only one who is going to accept me is you."

We looked at each other sadly.

"That's not so bad," he said. "I throw half of the parties anyway."

"That's true. And all the ones that are worthwhile." I held his hand.

"Isobel, look over there," said Monching. Paulo was standing alone at the edge of the garden. He was walking suspiciously in circles, then he disappeared into the trees.

"Go," said Monching. "I'm sure he wants you to follow him."

"Are you sure?"

"What else would he be doing?" Monching pushed me in the direction of the trees. Uncertainly, I set out across the lawn. I didn't want to talk to Paulo, especially not now, but for some reason, I didn't feel that I had a choice. I took a deep breath, and then walked into the trees. It was dark, but not dark enough. The sun still managed to break through the leaves. I looked at my arm, bare except for the patterns made by the shadowy lacework of vines and leaves, and standing beneath a tree, a smile on his face, was Paulo.

"Isobel, come here," he said. He wanted me, there in the trees, but I felt scared. "I played a song for you. 'J'ai deux amours.' Did you hear it?"

"I heard it."

"What's the matter?" he said. He sensed something was wrong. "I won't see you for two weeks. That's a long time. Come closer."

I looked down at the ground, the leaves, the vines. "This is wrong," I said. "This is your wedding."

"So what?" He smiled. "Antonia's in the house. She's having trouble with her rash. She won't know."

I looked over my shoulder.

"Isobel, there's no one there."

"There might be. Someone could be watching."

"No one's watching." I didn't move. "Isobel, I like

your dress," he said. "White. I knew you'd wear white."

"I thought it appropriate," I said.

"Yes," he agreed. "Try to think of this as your wedding, too." He started walking toward me, through the trees, pushing the bushes and vines aside. He moved quietly, smoothly, almost gliding along the ground.

"Paulo, stop," I said. "I don't want this."

"What do you mean?"

"I don't . . ." I couldn't think of what to say. I wanted him to stay away from me. "I don't like you."

"Of course you don't. Why would you?" He smiled. "I just married someone else. You're angry now, but in time you'll soften. I know you understand."

"I'm going home now."

"Home? Where is your home?" He was confused, getting angry. "Your home is here, because I'm here. Your home is with me."

"No." I was getting flustered. "I don't want you. I don't want to see you anymore."

"It's a little late for that, isn't it? What do you have without me? You have no money, no family who's willing to claim you. You're just resentful of Antonia now."

"No, I'm not," I said, interrupting. "I'm not resentful. I don't feel that. I don't feel anything anymore."

"What?" He smiled, superior. "Have you had an emotional lobotomy since I last saw you?"

"I think so," I said. He came closer. I stepped back into a thorny bush. My dress was caught. I tried to free it without tearing it.

"There you are," he said. "How convenient. Caught in a bush." He moved closer.

"Don't," I said. I stepped back quickly, tearing my dress.

"Now look," he said, "was that absolutely necessary?"

"My dress, it's torn," I said. Everything started to become clear. "My dress is torn, and you're the snake, just as it was in the dream."

"Isobel, what are you babbling about?"

I heard a twig snap, some distance away. I froze. "We're being watched," I said.

"Watched?" Paulo's patience had worn thin. "By who?"

"Gregorio," I whispered. "He's going to kill me."

"I've had about enough of this," said Paulo.

I turned and ran. I pushed through the webs and vines, branches, trying to get to the light of the garden, where all was safe. I broke through the trees at the edge, but someone followed close behind, someone who wasn't Paulo. He came out of the trees about five meters from where I stood. It was Gregorio. He had a gun. I stood watching him, but said nothing. I couldn't. I just watched him as he struggled with himself to raise the gun. I calmly waited for the shot that would take me away from Paulo, away from the world that I had created for myself. I craved the sound of the gunshot, the sight of a bullet moving through the air toward me. I looked into Gregorio's watery brown eyes. He seemed so strong, freed from all his troubled thoughts. He breathed uneasily, letting the gun raise itself level with my head. But then he faltered. He let the gun fall to his side, crying, helpless; then he raised it to his own head, and quickly pulled the trigger.

"No!" I screamed, with the gun, both noises tearing through the air as Gregorio fell softly onto the grass. I walked toward him, aware of nothing. I walked over and knelt on the grass, lifting his head into my lap, onto my white dress. It was as if a child, or a helpless animal, had died. And I knew that I had killed him. I was as guilty as if I myself had pulled the trigger. I stroked his soft brown hair, now warm with blood. I gently closed his eyes, then put my hand beneath his chin, closing his mouth. He could have been asleep, or resting. I took his hand, the one that had held the gun. It was warmer than mine.

"Isobel, come away from him," said Paulo. But I wouldn't, I couldn't leave him. Paulo came over and held my shoulders.

"Come on. Get up," he said.

"Leave me alone."

"Isobel, you don't even know him," Paulo said.

"I killed him, Paulo. I killed him."

"Don't be ridiculous."

"I killed him, and I killed my mother."

"She's hysterical," he said to the crowd that had gathered around us. "She's been under a lot of pressure lately."

He took my arm, tried to pull me away. I jerked back from him. My hands were covered with blood.

"All right," Paulo said. "I'll let you sit there until the ambulance arrives."

"He's dead, Paulo," I said. What was the use of an ambulance for a dead person? I looked at the crowd around me. Some people were crying, others held each other, everyone seemed frightened, but I recognized no one. It was as if they were all the same person repeated over and over, and I was alone, in the center. Gregorio's hand was cooler now, almost as cool as my mother's. I let it drop onto the grass. It was white, with short clean nails and long slender fingers. His eyes were closed, and his mouth was beginning to hold shut. He looked so peaceful, as if he was just sleeping. I envied him, because no one could disturb him. He would lie this way forever.

I envied him lying there. It was as if he was the gibbon, now freed, unchained from his troubled guilt and whatever thoughts he had of me. I held his hand, the well-groomed fingers with short, clean nails. I felt something for him, which I couldn't place as anything but need or love. It was a need to love things that couldn't love me back, a need to love things that would soon be cold.

TITLES OF THE AVAILABLE PRESS
in order of publication

THE CENTAUR IN THE GARDEN, a novel by Moacyr Scliar*
EL ANGEL'S LAST CONQUEST, a novel by Elvira Orphée
A STRANGE VIRUS OF UNKNOWN ORIGIN, a study by Dr. Jacques Leibowitch
THE TALES OF PATRICK MERLA, short stories by Patrick Merla
ELSEWHERE, a novel by Jonathan Strong*
THE AVAILABLE PRESS/PEN SHORT STORY COLLECTION
CAUGHT, a novel by Jane Schwartz*
THE ONE MAN ARMY, a novel by Moacyr Scliar
THE CARNIVAL OF THE ANIMALS, short stories by Moacyr Scliar
LAST WORDS AND OTHER POEMS, poetry by Antler
O'CLOCK, short stories by Quim Monzó
MURDER BY REMOTE CONTROL, a novel in pictures by Janwillem van de Wetering and Paul Kirchner
VIC HOLYFIELD AND THE CLASS OF 1957, a novel by William Heyen*
AIR, a novel by Michael Upchurch
THE GODS OF RAQUEL, a novel by Moacyr Scliar*
SUTERISMS, pictures by David Suter
DOCTOR WOOREDDY'S PRESCRIPTION FOR ENDURING THE END OF THE WORLD, a novel by Colin Johnson
THE CHESTNUT RAIN, a poem by William Heyen
THE MAN IN THE MONKEY SUIT, a novel by Oswaldo França Júnior
KIDDO, a novel by David Handler*
COD STREUTH, a novel by Bamber Gascoigne
LUNACY & CAPRICE, a novel by Henry Van Dyke
HE DIED WITH HIS EYES OPEN, a mystery by Derek Raymond*
DUSTSHIP GLORY, a novel by Andreas Schroeder
FOR LOVE, ONLY FOR LOVE, a novel by Pasquale Festa Campanile
'BUCKINGHAM PALACE,' DISTRICT SIX, a novel by Richard Rive
THE SONG OF THE FOREST, a novel by Colin Mackay*
BE-BOP, RE BOP, a novel by Xam Wilson Cartier
THE DEVIL'S HOME ON LEAVE, a mystery by Derek Raymond*
THE BALLAD OF THE FALSE MESSIAH, a novel by Moacyr Scliar
little pictures, short stories by Andrew Ramer
THE IMMIGRANT: A Hamilton County Album, a play by Mark Harelik
HOW THE DEAD LIVE, a mystery by Derek Raymond*
BOSS, a novel by David Handler*

THE TUNNEL, a novel by Ernesto Sábato
THE FOREIGN STUDENT, a novel by Philippe Labro, translated by William R. Byron
ARLISS, a novel by Llyla Allen
THE CHINESE WESTERN: Short Fiction from Today's China, translated by Zhu Hong
THE VOLUNTEERS, a novel by Moacyr Scliar
LOST SOULS, a novel by Anthony Schmitz
SEESAW MILLIONS, a novel by Janwillem van de Wetering
SWEET DIAMOND DUST, a novel by Rosario Ferré
SMOKEHOUSE JAM, a novel by Lloyd Little
THE ENIGMATIC EYE, short stories by Moacyr Scliar
THE WAY IT HAPPENS IN NOVELS, a novel by Kathleen O'Connor
THE FLAME FOREST, a novel by Michael Upchurch
FAMOUS QUESTIONS, a novel by Fanny Howe
SON OF TWO WORLDS, a novel by Haydn Middleton
WITHOUT A FARMHOUSE NEAR, nonfiction by Deborah Rawson
THE RATTLESNAKE MASTER, a novel by Beaufort Cranford
BENEATH THE WATERS, a novel by Oswaldo França Júnior
AN AVAILABLE MAN, a novel by Patric Kuh
THE HOLLOW DOLL (*A Little Box of Japanese Shocks*), by William Bohnaker
MAX AND THE CATS, a novel by Moacyr Scliar
FLIEGELMAN'S DESIRE, a novel by Lewis Buzbee
SLOW BURN, a novel by Sabina Murray
THE CARNAL PRAYER MAT, a novel by Li Yu, translated from the Chinese by Patrick Hanan

*Available in a Ballantine Mass Market Edition.